Longarm ate quickly so that he cou̲_____
the same time as the others. He didn't want to delay the
stage. Cougar put on a battered old hat with a pushed-up
brim and went out to see that the fresh team was hitched
up to his liking. Longarm hadn't spoken to the other passengers, but he gave the two drummers a polite nod. The
other two men still seemed to be ignoring him. They pushed
back from the table and went outside, causing Longarm to
frown slightly. If he'd had his druthers, he would have liked
to get outside before the two hardcases. Stepping from a
lighted room into darkness could be dangerous if somebody
who wanted to kill you was lurking in the shadows.

He stood up, pushed aside the empty bowl and plate,
dropped a coin beside them to pay for the meal, and turned
toward the door. Behind him, the two drummers talked and
laughed in low tones.

Longarm was almost to the door when a voice said behind him, "All right, Long, that's far enough. Stand right
there and put up your hands."

The unmistakable sound of two guns being cocked punctuated the order.

TABOR EVANS

LONGARM

AND THE BANK
ROBBER'S DAUGHTER

JOVE BOOKS, NEW YORK

This is a work of fiction. Names, characters, places, and incidents either are the product of the author's imagination or are used fictitiously, and any resemblance to actual persons, living or dead, business establishments, events, or locales is entirely coincidental.

LONGARM AND THE BANK ROBBER'S DAUGHTER

A Jove Book / published by arrangement with
the author

PRINTING HISTORY
Jove edition / December 2003

ISBN: 0-515-13641-7

A JOVE BOOK®
Jove Books are published by The Berkley Publishing Group, a division of Penguin Group (USA) Inc., 375 Hudson Street, New York, New York 10014. JOVE and the "J" design are trademarks belonging to Penguin Group (USA) Inc.

PRINTED IN THE UNITED STATES OF AMERICA

10 9 8 7 6 5 4 3 2 1

Chapter 1

Longarm jerked open the door of his rented room and growled, "What the hell do you want?"

Then his jaw tightened as he realized that Death had come knocking on this mild spring evening in Denver.

Death wore the pale, haggard face of an old man who clutched at his middle. Crimson blood welled between the fingers of the hands he pressed against his belly. He leaned forward and croaked, "G-Gold . . ."

Longarm reached out a hand to steady the old man. Iron-hard fingers closed around a thin, palsied upper arm. "Hang on, old-timer," he said. "Let's get you set down, and then I'll fetch a sawbones."

The old man lifted his other arm and waved a gnarled hand covered with blood. "No . . . time . . . all that gold . . . stolen gold . . ." His voice grew weaker and he sagged forward, closer to Longarm, and looked up from haunted eyes. He gasped, "Sweetwater Canyon!"

Then from the landing down at the other end of the hall, a gun blared. The heavy slug smashed into the old man and drove him forward into the big lawman's arms. Behind Longarm, Miss Alice Monaghan let out a frightened scream as Longarm stumbled backward, hugging the

1

blood-drenched form of his unexpected visitor.

Well, thought Longarm, *this* evening sure as hell wasn't turning out the way he had hoped it would.

It began with a good meal in a decent but not overly expensive restaurant down the street from the boarding house where Longarm lived. When he went in, the only hunger he was interested in satisfying was the one in his belly. But when he smiled at the pretty, redheaded, green-eyed girl on the other side of the room and she smiled back at him, other ideas popped into his head.

Before the meal was over, they were sitting at the same table. Longarm wasn't quite sure if it had been his idea or hers. What mattered was that they got along just fine. Her name was Alice Monaghan, and she was on her way to San Francisco to live with her aunt and uncle. Her parents back east had died recently, and although Alice was twenty-two years old and perfectly capable of living on her own, her aunt and uncle wouldn't hear of it. Why, it just wouldn't be proper for an unmarried young woman to live alone, they wrote to her.

She explained all that to Longarm, then said, "I'm afraid the poor old dears have a rather inflated idea of just how proper I am." Those Irish eyes of hers twinkled when she said it.

Longarm had been flirted with by the best. He prided himself on his ability to tell when a gal was just flirting for the fun of it and that was all, and when she had something more serious in mind. Alice Monaghan was enjoying herself, all right, but she wanted more than that. She confirmed Longarm's opinion by nodding eagerly when he suggested that they go back to his room for a drink.

He preferred Maryland rye himself, Tom Moore if he could get it, but he sometimes kept a bottle of brandy in his room for when his ladyfriends came to call. Tonight, after they had walked arm in arm to the boarding house with Alice so close beside him that Longarm could feel the soft, warm pressure of her breast, he had poured her a healthy dollop of the brandy and one for himself, too. They sat on the bed and sipped the smooth, warm liquor, and then Longarm kissed her. He tasted the brandy as he slipped his tongue into her mouth. She took hold of his hand and moved it to her breast. What with the traveling outfit she wore and all the feminine stays and laces and such-like under it, he couldn't get all that good of a feel. But he liked what he felt, anyway. He liked it even more when she reached down and brushed the back of her hand across the growing bulge in his britches. Her tongue danced hotly and wetly around his, and he thought that this was going to turn out to be a mighty pleasurable evening.

Then somebody started pounding on the door . . .

Longarm caught his balance, driving the heels of his boots against the planks of the floor. A ghastly rattle sounded right beside his ear as the old-timer's head flopped forward. The dead weight Longarm was supporting became even deader. The old man was a goner.

Alice screamed again as Longarm twisted around and tossed the body on the bed beside her. He didn't much blame her for jamming her hands in her mouth and scooting up against the headboard to get away from the corpse. That caterwauling was starting to get a mite annoying, though.

He reached over to palm the Colt 45 out of the cross-draw rig on his left hip and said, "Better get on the floor, just in case." Bullets fired in the haste of a gunfight usually tended to go a little high. He turned toward the door.

It was open and empty. Whoever had shot the old man was either still out there in the corridor or had taken off for the tall and uncut. Longarm glanced over his shoulder and saw that Alice had taken his advice, throwing herself

3

face down on the floor beside the bed. He went through the door in a crouch, swiveling toward the landing, the gun in his hand tracking from left to right, seeking a target.

The hall was empty, and so was the landing at the end.

Longarm drew a deep breath. He didn't know who the old man was, didn't know who had shot him or why. But the man had been on Longarm's doorstep when he was gunned down, and he had died while Longarm was holding him. That made it personal, no matter what the reasons behind the shooting.

He ran down the hall to the stairs, took them three at a time as he headed down to the ground floor. A traveling salesman in a gaudy checked suit gaped at him from the entrance to the parlor. "Which way did the son of a bitch go?" Longarm snapped at the drummer.

"Out . . . out the back!" The salesman pointed with a quavering finger to the rear hall. Longarm went that way. "But there were two of them!" the drummer called after him.

That made things a little more dicey, thought Longarm. There had been only one shot, so he had hoped there was only one shooter. But he had known from the start that he might be pursuing more than one man. He knew as well that they probably had horses stashed behind the house for a getaway. If that was the case, he had only seconds to catch up to them before they fogged it away from the place.

He burst out the rear door, and as he did, a bullet screamed out of the night and chewed splinters from the jamb near his head. Three wooden steps led down to the ground. Longarm ignored them and went off the top step in a rolling dive. More shots rang out as he hit the ground. One of the bullets sprayed dirt in his face. He spat grit out of his mouth as he came to a stop on his belly and triggered twice toward the spot where he had seen the orange flare of a muzzle blast. Somebody yelled in pain.

Longarm surged to his feet, darted to his right, then his left as he charged forward. Colt flame bloomed again in the darkness ahead of him. Something that sounded like an angry hornet buzzed past his ear. He returned the fire.

"Damn it!" rasped a man's voice that was filled with anger and frustration. A swift rataplan of hoofbeats followed on the heels of the curse. Longarm weaved and went to a knee behind a rain barrel beside the privy as two guns opened up on him, the shots angling in toward him. Given the hoofbeats and the fact that he was still facing two enemies, he figured the horses belonging to the gunmen had been spooked by all the shooting and had broken loose and bolted, leaving the Coltmen afoot. That would make them more eager than ever to kill Longarm.

The rooming house was only a few blocks from downtown Denver, but Cherry Creek ran behind it and there were some trees and open ground back here. If the two men split up, Longarm couldn't go after both of them. For the time being, though, they seemed to have given up on the idea of flight. Instead, they were trying to shoot the rain barrel to pieces. Longarm hunkered as low as he could while bullets thudded into the barrel. The water inside the barrel stopped the slugs from going all the way through. But as the shots died away for a second, probably while the killers reloaded, Longarm heard the sound of water trickling out of the barrel through the holes that had been punched in it by the hail of lead. Pretty soon the water would all leak out, and then he'd be in trouble.

He didn't wait for that to happen. He straightened and kicked the barrel over, sending the rest of the water sloshing out. Another kick sent the barrel rolling toward the gunmen, who had taken cover in some trees on the creek bank. Longarm went to his left as the shooters reacted instinctively and burned more powder by firing at the rolling barrel instead of him. By the time they switched their

5

aim, he was in thick darkness himself, crouched in another clump of trees.

Longarm stayed motionless for a moment and caught his breath, dragging the night air into his lungs. He heard the shrill sound of police whistles in the distance. They came closer by the second. The Denver police, efficient when they wanted to be, were on the way. Nobody could fight a small-scale war only a short distance from downtown without the local defenders of law and order knowing about it. Pretty soon the whole area behind the boarding house would be blanketed with blue-uniformed, copper-buttoned, badge toters.

Longarm knew that, and so did the two men he was after. They broke from cover, going different directions. One of them tried to splash straight across the creek. Longarm fired at the sound and was rewarded by a gurgling cry of agony and a bigger splash. The other man threw some wild shots at him and made him duck. Longarm went after him, racing along the bank of the creek, darting around trees and bushes.

Enthusiasm got the best of him. Longarm knew the man might double back, but he didn't really think that would happen. His quarry seemed to be fleeing in panic, desperate not to be caught. So Longarm wasn't quite as careful as he should have been and didn't know for sure that the gunman was waiting for him until the fella came hurtling out of some bushes to crash into him.

The impact of the collision drove Longarm off his feet. His instincts and quick reflexes allowed him to twist somewhat in midair so that he hit the ground beside the man who had tackled him, rather than underneath him.

He still had one cartridge in the cylinder of the Colt, but before he could bring the revolver to bear, a hand locked around the wrist of his gun hand and forced it to the ground. The man's other hand found Longarm's neck and fastened on it in a death grip.

The gunman must have run out of bullets and hadn't had time to reload before springing his ambush. That thought flickered through the back of Longarm's brain. He was mostly concerned, though, with the fact that the air was shut off from his lungs. He'd been caught between breaths, so it wasn't long before things started to get a mite hazy. The night seemed to fill with a red mist that swirled around the dark, bulky figure looming halfway over him. Longarm tried to lift his gun arm, but the man's weight pinned it to the ground.

The hombre had two arms, though, not three, and he couldn't hold Longarm's gun hand, strangle him, and ward off blows from Longarm's other hand all at the same time. Longarm brought his left fist around in a short, hooking punch that smashed into the side of his opponent's head.

The man grunted in pain but held on. His grip loosened slightly, though. Longarm hit him again, then bucked up off the ground, arching his back. He twisted his shoulders and his neck came free from the man's choking fingers. He gasped for air.

His gun hand was still pinned to the ground. The killer grabbed Longarm's wrist with both hands and tried to shake the revolver free. Longarm reached up, closed his fingers on the man's collar, and hauled him over as he turned. Both men rolled over, and now the Colt was between them. Without warning, the gun bucked in Longarm's hand, but the roar of the shot was muffled by flesh pressed against the barrel. Instead of continuing to struggle with Longarm, the man spasmed and jerked back. He started to flop around on the ground like a fish out of water. Even in the dim light, the sight was a grotesque one to Longarm's eyes.

The man's horrible writhing lasted only a couple of seconds. Then a sigh escaped from him and he lay back, motionless except for a slight jerking of his legs that lasted a few more heartbeats. He grew still as his muscles and nerves realized the same thing Longarm already knew. The second gunman was dead.

Longarm climbed to his feet. Without really thinking about it, he opened the Colt's cylinder, shook out the empty shells, and thumbed fresh cartridges into the gun after taking them from his coat pocket. Then he snapped the cylinder closed.

Heavy footsteps sounded behind him, and the beam of light from a bull's-eye lantern played over his tall, rangy form. "Hold it right there, mister!" a harsh voice ordered. "You're covered! Drop that gun!"

Turning his head so that he could speak over his shoulder, he said, "I ain't in the habit of dropping my gun on the ground, Fluharty. Ain't good for it."

"Long? That you? Turn around slow-like, and keep them hands where we can see 'em."

Longarm followed those orders. He squinted against the glare of the light that one of the policemen shined in his eyes.

" 'Tis Marshal Long all right, boys. Culverhouse, stop shinin' that damned lantern in his face."

Longarm nodded his thanks as the blinding light dropped toward the ground. He had known Officer Fluharty for quite some time and was on good terms with the man. Unlike some of the other members of the Denver police force, Fluharty didn't resent the federal lawmen who worked out of the big building on Colfax Avenue.

"What in blue blazes happened here, Long?" asked Fluharty. "Who's the stiff?"

"I don't rightly know," Longarm replied, "but there may be another one over yonder in the creek. Why don't you leave a couple of your boys here, and we'll go take a look."

"All right, come along. Burke, Henderson, you two stay here with this corpse."

Longarm walked toward Cherry Creek with the burly policeman. Two more officers trailed behind them, one carrying the lantern. He tried to angle the beam of light so that it would illuminate the ground in front of Longarm and Fluharty, but they walked too fast for that. Both men had keen eyes and didn't really need the light.

Sure enough, a couple of minutes later Longarm and Fluharty found another body floating in the creek, hung up in the shallows along the bank. Fluharty reached out and got hold of the corpse, dragged the dripping figure up onto the grass. The policeman with the light shined it on the dead man's face.

It was the countenance of a typical hardcase, lean and sharp, sporting a couple of days' beard stubble. He was dressed in range clothes. Longarm had never seen him before, at least not that he could recollect, and he had a good memory for faces. He hunkered on his heels next to the corpse and picked up the man's right hand.

"Enough calluses in the right places to show that the fella did some cowboying. But I figure he threw a gun a lot more often than he ever did a rope."

"You know him?" asked Fluharty.

"Nope."

"Got any idea why he wanted to kill you?"

Longarm straightened. "You're jumping to conclusions, old son. These two didn't try to bushwhack me."

"They didn't?" Fluharty sounded surprised. "Then why did you shoot them?"

"Oh, they did their level best to ventilate my hide," Longarm said. "But not until after they'd gunned down somebody else and I went after 'em for it."

"Another killing, you say?" The big policeman shook his head. " 'Tis a pity what this town is comin' to."

Longarm didn't waste time pointing out that Denver was a lot more calm and civilized these days than it had been the first time he'd seen it, before he'd ever started packing a star for Uncle Sam's Justice Department. Instead, he said, "Let's take a look at the other one, make sure he's a stranger, too."

It required only a minute to determine that Longarm's hunch was correct. The second gunman was just as unknown to him as the first one. The man was the same sort, not totally unaccustomed to ranch work but with the look of the owlhoot trails about him. The shot that Longarm had inadvertently fired into his midsection had torn through his belly and blown his spine in half as it came out his back.

"You said somebody *else* got shot?" Fluharty prodded.

Longarm inclined his head toward the boarding house. "Inside." He led the way, anxious to make sure that Alice Monaghan was all right. No reason she shouldn't be, he thought. Except for the one shot that had hit the old man, all of tonight's gun music had been played outside.

Alice started down the stairs just as Longarm started up. Her face was pale, her eyes still wide with fear. She caught her breath and drew back a little at the sight of him. He glanced down at himself and saw that the front of his coat was smeared with blood from when he'd grabbed hold of the old man.

"I'm s-sorry, Custis," Alice said. "I . . . I have to catch a train . . ."

Earlier in the evening, she hadn't been worried about laying over for the night and taking the next westbound in the morning. But that was before guns started going off and old codgers covered with blood got dropped on the bed beside her. Longarm didn't really blame her for not feeling romantic anymore.

"You're not hurt?" he asked her in a low voice.

"I'm fine. I just . . ." She stopped, looked up at him for a second, and asked, "Do things like this happen to you very often?"

He nodded solemnly and replied, "I'm sad to say they do."

She moved past him and Fluharty, and went down the stairs. Longarm cast one regretful glance over his shoulder at her, then climbed up to the second floor and stalked along the hall to his room.

The old geezer was right where Longarm had left him, which came as no surprise. He was too dead to go anywhere under his own power. In a few terse sentences, Longarm explained to the policeman what had happened, omitting a detailed description of how he and Alice had been sitting on the bed kissing and fondling each other. He didn't mention the few last words the codger had spoken, either.

"I suppose this old fella's just as much a stranger to you as those two other men were," Fluharty said.

Longarm studied the old man's face. It was lean, hollow-cheeked, pale. The pallor was so deep that it could have resulted from something besides just the loss of blood from his wounds. The man's hair was thin and mostly white. White bristles stood out on his chin and cheeks. His neck was stringy. He wore a cheap coat and trousers and a white shirt. The clothes were dirty but seemed to be fairly new. So were his shoes. Longarm checked his pockets, found nothing except a couple of wadded-up greenback dollars.

"Never saw him before," Longarm said, "but if you want to know who he is, I'd start by checking with the prisons. He looks like he's been behind bars for quite a spell and just got out not long ago."

Fluharty frowned. "How do you figure that?"

Longarm gestured toward the old man's face. "That's a prison pallor he's sporting if I've ever seen. And that suit of clothes he's wearing looks like what convicts are issued when they're released. You can send word to the Colorado state pen at Canon City, and I'll have the marshal's office wire his description to Leavenworth and the other state prisons in these parts. There's really no telling where he came from, but he looks like he hasn't been out for long. Chances are he didn't come too far."

"I reckon you're probably right," Fluharty said. One of the other policemen clumped into the room, and Fluharty turned to ask him, "Did you have those bodies hauled along to the morgue?"

The officer nodded. "That's right. We searched them first before the meat wagon came for them."

"What did you find?" asked Longarm. He would have been willing to bet that a search of the dead men's pockets hadn't turned up much.

"Nothing to identify them. Each of them had a hundred bucks in gold double eagles on them."

Longarm nodded. The money had to be the pay-off for the killing of the old man, or at least a down payment on the job.

"We'll spread their descriptions around, see if we can find anybody willin' to admit to knowin' them," Fluharty said. "I don't hold out much hope of that happenin', though."

"Neither do I," Longarm agreed. "They were just hired guns." He looked at the body on the bed. "If there were any real answers, this old son here is the one who had them. And he ain't talking."

Chapter 2

When he came into the outer office of Chief Marshal Billy Vail the next morning, Longarm paused just inside the door, took off his flat-crowned, snuff-brown Stetson, and sailed it with practiced ease onto one of the brass hooks on the hat tree.

Henry, the bespectacled young fella who played the typewriter for Vail, looked up from his desk and asked, "What time were you here last night, anyway?"

"I reckon it was about ten o'clock," Longarm said. "I got the watchman to let me in. You found the note I left?"

Henry nodded. "Yes, and I sent those wires you asked me to, first thing this morning."

"Much obliged. Any replies yet?"

Henry sniffed. "As you know, I always get here early—*considerably* earlier than some I could name—but even so, there hasn't been time yet for any replies to have arrived. I'll let you know as soon as they do." The young man inclined his head toward the door behind him. "I assume you want to see Marshal Vail?"

"I figured Billy and me would chew the fat for a while, yeah."

"Go ahead. He's anxious to hear all about your little

adventure last night There's already a report on his desk from the Denver Police Department about it."

Henry sounded a mite too happy about that, thought Longarm. Any time Henry was happy, it didn't bode well. Longarm went to the door of Billy Vail's private office, opened it, and went inside.

The chief marshal glanced up from his paper-littered desk. "I thought I heard your voice out there, Custis. Come in and have a seat."

Longarm closed the door behind him and stepped over to the red leather chair in front of Vail's desk. The chief marshal—short, pudgy, balding, and pink-cheeked—had the look of a cherub about him, but when Billy Vail was on a tear, people forgot all about his appearance. Vail had spent his life in law enforcement, including a stint with the legendary Texas Rangers. He had been a ring-tailed hell-roarer in his time, and he still had plenty of bark on him even though he was mostly confined to a desk these days. The gaze he turned on Longarm was cold and angry.

Longarm glanced at the banjo clock on the wall. It wasn't even nine-thirty yet. For him, that was pretty early, so Vail couldn't be upset about the hour. Longarm started to fish a cheroot out of his vest pocket, saying, "I reckon Henry told you—"

"He did," Vail cut in, "and so did the Denver Police Department." He picked up a couple of sheets of paper from the welter on his desk. "Three dead men in less than a quarter of an hour."

Longarm fiddled with the cheroot in his hand. "Yeah, but to be fair about it, I only killed two of them," he pointed out.

Vail rolled his eyes and tossed the documents back onto the desk. "I suppose that's true enough," he admitted. "But you can't deny that you seem to attract trouble, Custis. The police are getting tired of carting off your corpses for you."

14

Longarm snapped a lucifer into life and held the flame to the tip of the tightly rolled cheroot. When he had the smoke going, he shook out the match and dropped it on the floor beside the chair. "Then tell 'em to keep folks from murdering old codgers on my doorstep and trying to kill me," he suggested.

Vail sighed. "Tell me what happened. I read the police report and the note you left for Henry last night, but I want the details."

Longarm gave them to him, this time including the cryptic comments the dying old man had made about stolen gold. He concluded by saying, "Before you ask me, I don't have a notion in hell what it's all about, Billy. I'm hoping that if we can identify the old man, that'll put us on the right trail."

"How do you know there *is* a trail?" asked Vail.

"Well . . ." Longarm frowned in thought. He hadn't really expected that question. "There's got to be a reason that old-timer was so anxious to get to me and tell me about that gold. He'd already stopped a slug or two before he ever reached the boarding house. Just like there has to be a reason those two lobos came after him. They wanted to stop him from talking to me."

Vail's eyes narrowed as he looked across the desk at his chief deputy. "The old man was shot four times total, according to the coroner. How do you *know* he was coming to see you? Did he call you by name?"

Longarm's frown deepened. "Now that I think about it, I don't recollect that he did."

"So he might not have known who you are. He might've knocked on any door at random, trying to get away from those two gunmen."

Longarm chewed on the cheroot for a second, then leaned forward and said, "Hold on, Billy. That don't make sense. If he was just looking for a place to hide from them killers, why would he go to all the trouble of climbing the stairs to the second floor? Wouldn't he have stopped in the parlor, or the dining room, or one of the rooms on the ground floor?" Longarm shook his head. "Nope, he was looking for me particular-like. I'm convinced of it."

"But you can't prove it."

Longarm's shoulders rose and fell in a shrug. "I can't prove the world's round, neither, but that's what the teacher said in that ol' one-room schoolhouse back in West-by-God Virginia when I was a sprout."

Vail leaned back in his chair and rested his palms on the desk. "I'll admit that it looks like the old man was trying to get to you when he was shot," he said. "We don't know that it has anything to do with the business of this office, though. Maybe some old friend of yours asked him to look you up."

With a wry smile, Longarm said, "I don't have all that many friends in prison, Billy."

Vail poked the police report with a blunt finger. "I can understand from the man's description why you think he might've been a jailbird not long ago. But I still think you're just guessing about the other, Custis. Until we know for sure that this has something to do with a federal crime, I can't have you wasting your time investigating it."

"How'd you know that's what I figured to do?"

A short bark of laughter came from the chief marshal. "How long have you been working for me, Custis? By now I know the way that mind of yours works just as well as you do, if not better. A man gets killed right in front of you, and then the gunmen who did for him try to plug you as well when you go after them. You wouldn't be much of a lawdog if you didn't want to get to the bottom of that."

Longarm blew a perfect smoke ring and tried not to grin. Vail knew him all too well, he thought.

He was ready to argue the point when the door of the

inner office opened and Henry came in. The young man had a yellow telegraph flimsy in his hand. Thinking that it was a reply to one of the wires he'd had Henry send, Longarm reached for the piece of paper. Henry veered around him, keeping the flimsy out of reach, and placed it on Vail's desk.

"This was just delivered, Marshal," Henry said with a self-satisfied smirk at Longarm. "I knew you'd want to see it right away."

Longarm watched intently as Vail scanned the message printed on the paper. Vail glanced up, his eyes troubled, and Longarm knew his assumptions about the old codger and the two gunmen had been correct. "There is some connection between me and that old-timer, ain't there, Billy?" he asked. "I'd bet a hat on it."

"You'd have a new lid coming to you if you did," muttered Vail. "Maybe." He tossed the telegram across the desk where Longarm could reach it. "The federal penitentiary at Fort Leavenworth released a prisoner a week ago who matches the old man's description. His name was Floyd Pollard."

"Never heard of him," Longarm said as he picked up the yellow paper.

"His cellmate before he was released was—"

"Clete Harrigan," Longarm finished the sentence, reading the name off the telegram.

"I reckon you recall Harrigan."

"Damned right I do," Longarm said, his mouth tightening with remembered anger.

Several years earlier, Clete Harrigan had led a gang of bank robbers that had gone on a rampage of outlawry stretching from Idaho to New Mexico Territory. Frank and Jesse James and their cousins the Youngers got written up in the papers more, but the Harrigan Gang had been almost as prolific and efficient at looting banks. Longarm had been just one of hundreds of lawmen who had tried to track down Harrigan and his men. He'd been the one who succeeded, though. Not long after the Harrigan Gang pulled their biggest job yet, holding up a bank in western Kansas where an army payroll had been shipped prior to its disbursement, Longarm had cornered Clete Harrigan himself in a Raton whorehouse. The resulting exchange of bullets had left Harrigan with a busted shoulder. His gang hadn't been with him, but with the exception of his segundo, Matt Rainey, the other outlaws didn't amount to much. Harrigan was the brains and the driving force of the outfit. Rainey had been an able second-in-command, but that was all. With Harrigan safely behind bars, the gang's reign of terror was over.

The problem was that none of the loot they had stolen was ever recovered, especially that army payroll. Most of the rest undoubtedly had been spent already, but there hadn't been time to go through the gold double eagles that should have wound up in the pockets of several thousand cavalry troopers.

Longarm's brows drew down in a frown as he thought about the double eagles that had been found on the gunmen he'd killed. That could have been a coincidence, he told himself. There were plenty of twenty-dollar gold pieces floating around the West. And yet there was enough of a connection to the vanished payroll stolen by Clete Harrigan that Longarm couldn't help but wonder about it.

Harrigan had claimed that the gang hadn't split up the money yet when he was wounded and captured by Longarm. His story was that he had hidden the loot, and he wasn't going to say where. It was obvious he was trying to use the payroll as leverage to get himself a lighter sentence. The ploy hadn't worked. Several people had died from shots fired in the course of the gang's robberies, though no witnesses reported that Harrigan had fired any of the fatal bullets himself. For that reason, perhaps, when he was found guilty he was sentenced to life in the federal penitentiary at Fort Leavenworth, rather than being given a date with the hangman.

The Harrigan Gang's loot was never found.

All that history ran through Longarm's mind in a matter of seconds. Clete Harrigan was still in prison, but his cellmate had been released a week earlier. That former cellmate, Floyd Pollard, had showed up at Longarm's door already ventilated three times, and the fourth bullet had put him down for good. There had to be a reason for what had happened.

Longarm looked up from the telegraph flimsy in his hand and stared across the desk at Billy Vail. "Harrigan must have sent the old man to find me," he said. "He gave Pollard a message to deliver to me."

Vail's eyes narrowed as he said, "If I recall correctly, Harrigan had a message for you when he was carted off to prison for the rest of his life. He swore he'd settle the score with you somehow. Maybe Pollard came to kill you."

Longarm considered that possibility for a moment and then shook his head. "Not likely, Billy. Even before he was shot, Pollard must've been pretty feeble. I wouldn't be surprised if they let him out of prison because he didn't have long to live. I don't reckon he'd have had much of a chance against me. That ain't bragging, just being reasonable."

"Still, Harrigan may have figured that any chance was better than none."

"Maybe, but I don't believe it," Longarm said stubbornly. "I think all he wanted to do was tell me about that gold. And don't forget, he mentioned Sweetwater Canyon."

"Where's that?" Vail asked.

Longarm shook his head again. "Don't know, but I reckon it might be a good idea to find out."

Henry had stepped back after giving the telegram to Vail, but he had remained in the room for the discussion. Now he said, "I'll get our maps of the region, and we can take a look."

"That's a good idea," said Vail. "Bring them in here and spread them out on the table."

Henry fetched several rolled-up maps from a cabinet in the outer office. He unrolled them one at a time and spread them out on the long table that sat to one side in Vail's office. The three men stood around the table, leaning over to study the maps.

Henry was the one who spotted the place on a map of New Mexico Territory. He pointed and said, "There, on the west side of the Sangre de Cristos, near San Luis Valley."

Longarm looked closer, then shook his head. "That says Sweetwater City."

"Yes, but there's a creek that runs past the town out into the valley. I'll bet it's Sweetwater Creek and that it runs through Sweetwater Canyon."

"Well, maybe," Longarm said a frown. "The only other Sweetwaters I know of are both down in Texas, and there ain't a real canyon near either one of them. One of the places ain't even called Sweetwater anymore. It's Mobeetie now."

"I think Henry may be on to something," Vail said, causing the young man to smile with pleasure. Henry didn't come in for all that much praise from his boss. "Harrigan was in Raton when you caught up with him, Custis, and that's almost due east across the mountains from this Sweetwater City."

Longarm had to admit the chief marshal was right. He didn't like the idea that Henry had spotted the place before he did, but he didn't want to be petty about it, either. "Reckon the thing I need to do now is take a *paseo* down

20

there and have a look around. Could be that Harrigan's loot is stashed somewhere in that canyon."

"That's enough of a possibility that I think we can justify the time and expense involved. When you came in here this morning, Custis, I had in mind to send you on another job, but I've decided against that. If there's a chance you can recover the Harrigan Gang's loot, that's what I want you to do." Vail looked over at Henry. "Get Marshal Long's travel vouchers made out. Custis, you'll be on the first train to Pueblo. I reckon from there you'll have to rent a horse and ride through the mountains."

That would be a rugged ride, too, thought Longarm. The Sangre de Cristos might be the tail end of the Rockies, but they still had some good-sized mountains scattered among them, including Wheeler Peak, which was damned near as tall as the Tetons up in Wyoming. Luckily, Longarm knew of several passes that would get him over to the San Luis Valley. According to the map, Sweetwater City was right on the eastern edge of the valley, with the canyon—if there was one—running up into the mountains behind it.

He turned toward the door and started to follow Henry out of Vail's office. "I'll go throw my gear in my warbag," he said over his shoulder.

"Wait just a minute, Custis."

Longarm stopped and turned back. Vail had a worried frown on his face.

"It occurs to me," the chief marshal said, "that this could be a trap. Maybe Harrigan didn't send Pollard to kill you. Maybe the old man was just the bait to get you to go down to Sweetwater Canyon. Once you get there, somebody else could be waiting to ambush you."

"I reckon you could be right." Longarm's cheroot had gone out while he and Vail and Henry were studying the maps, but he still had the butt in his hand. He put it in his mouth now, clenched his teeth, and said around it,

21

"But there's only one way to find out, Billy." He chuckled. "Won't be the first time I've had a target painted on my back."

Dryly, Vail said, "Let's hope it won't be the last."

Chapter 3

Packing his gear didn't take very long. A spare shirt and a set of long underwear, a couple of boxes of cartridges, a bottle of Maryland rye, his Winchester, and the McClellan saddle he favored for riding . . . That was all Longarm needed.

He took off his brown tweed suit, his vest, the string tie, and the boiled white shirt, replacing them with denim trousers, a butternut-colored cotton shirt with a bibbed front, and a dark brown bandanna around his neck. His denim jacket went in the warbag with the rest of the gear. Even at Denver's elevation, at this time of year it was warm enough most days that he didn't need the jacket, but it would be cooler in the mountains, especially at night.

He was just about set when a knock sounded on the door of his room.

Longarm frowned at the door. The last time someone had knocked on it, all sorts of commotion had been the result. This time, though, it wasn't a frantic pounding that summoned him. It was a more normal knock. He buckled on his gunbelt and went to the door, called through the panel, "Who is it?" Then he took a step to the side just in case somebody opened up with a greener, aiming to blast him through the door.

"Marshal Long? Marshal Custis Long?"

The voice belonged to a woman. Longarm frowned. He couldn't place it. As far as he could tell from the voice, the woman was a stranger. The question she asked confirmed that. She didn't know him, either.

Of course, some women could use a gun just about as well as a man. Longarm kept his right hand poised near the butt of the Colt as he twisted the knob and pulled the door open. If his visitor was out for trouble, he'd just have to oblige her.

She didn't look like a troublemaker, though, he saw instantly. She was tall, with a slender, coltish figure in a gray wool traveling dress that hugged her body in the right places. Short blond hair curled out from under a gray hat, and blue eyes regarded Longarm with a level, appraising stare. She held a neat, stylish bag in her hands, not a gun, as she said again, "Marshal Long?"

If she noticed that he was ready to throw down on her, she didn't give any sign of it.

As unobtrusively as possible, Longarm moved his hand away from the butt of his gun. "That's right, ma'am," he said with a nod. "What can I do for you?"

Her gaze stayed just as forthright as before as she said, "My name is Emily Harrigan."

Longarm knew that such things as coincidences existed, but he didn't put much stock in them. A lawman developed a healthy skepticism if he wanted to stay alive. So he didn't think this young woman's last name was any coincidence. Still, he didn't want to spook her before she revealed what she wanted, so he just nodded and said noncommittally, "Yes, ma'am?"

She was a cool one; he had to give her that. She said, "I believe you're acquainted with my father. His name is Clete Harrigan."

"I reckon we've met," Longarm said cautiously.

Emily Harrigan smiled then. "Why don't you invite me in, Marshal? I'm well aware of the history between you and my father, but I assure you, I didn't come here to try to take any sort of vengeance on you. Just the opposite, in fact. I owe you a debt of thanks."

Longarm was curious enough that he stepped back and motioned for her to come in. She did so, moving with a quiet grace that Longarm found very appealing.

"I can't offer much in the way of fancy," he said. "I'm on the trail a lot of the time. This is just where I hang my hat between jobs."

"This is fine," Emily Harrigan said as she settled down on the room's single straight-backed chair. She nodded toward the door, which Longarm was still holding open. "You can close that. I don't mind. I'm not worried about keeping up proper appearances. That would be a foolish concern for a bank robber's daughter, don't you think?"

The words had a brittle, self-mocking quality to them. Longarm eased the door shut, then crossed his arms and leaned a hip against the tall wardrobe across from the bed. "Just what is it I can do for you, Miss Harrigan?" he asked bluntly. "Is this about Floyd Pollard?"

The question wasn't really a shot in the dark. In less than twelve hours, he'd had two visitors here at his boarding house, both of them connected to Clete Harrigan. Those visits had to be hitched together. But as he watched Emily Harrigan, he saw her eyes widen with surprise, and her lips parted slightly as she caught her breath. "What about Floyd?" she asked sharply.

"You know he was here last night." Longarm's words were a statement, not a question.

Emily shook her head. "No, of course not. How could I know? The last time I saw Floyd, he . . . he was in . . ."

"Prison?" Longarm finished for her when she seemed unable or unwilling to go on.

25

Emily's chin lifted, and she sat a little straighter as her back stiffened. "That's right. There's no point in denying it. We both know my father is in Leavenworth Prison, and Floyd Pollard was his cellmate until recently. I know it because I visited them a couple of weeks ago. You know it, Marshal, because you put Clete Harrigan there, behind bars."

It wasn't in Longarm's nature to argue with a pretty gal, but some things, he just couldn't let pass. "The way I see it," he drawled, "it was your pa robbing all those banks that really put him behind bars."

She met his gaze squarely, her eyes full of defiance for a moment. But then a dull acceptance crept into them, and she sighed. "You're right, of course. Father was an outlaw. I've known that for years. Even when I was in school back east and told all the other young ladies that he was a mining tycoon, I knew he was really a criminal."

That explained why Longarm hadn't known anything about Harrigan having a daughter. More than one Westerner, law-abiding and otherwise, had family back east. Evidently Harrigan had sent his daughter to an exclusive school for young ladies, probably with a highfalutin' name like Miss Abigail's or some such, and no doubt part of the loot from the gang's bank robberies had gone to pay for it. But that didn't explain what Emily Harrigan was doing here now, or why she had shown up in Denver—and on Longarm's very doorstep—so soon after the eventful visit of her father's old cellmate.

After a moment's poignant silence, Longarm said, "I don't mean to rush you, ma'am, but I've got a heap on my plate just now. If you could just tell me what you're doing here . . . ?"

Again she looked up at him with a trace of defiance in her eyes. "I came to ask you if you've received a message from my father in the past few days. When I visited him at Leavenworth two weeks ago, I urged him to get in

26

touch with you. I thought that as a lawman, you might be able to help him."

Longarm's interest intensified. Here was a possible explanation for Floyd Pollard coming to see him. What Emily had just said made it more likely than ever that Pollard had been carrying a message to Longarm from Clete Harrigan.

Avoiding a direct answer, Longarm said, "That old fella Pollard showed up here last night. Maybe your pa sent him."

"Is he still here?" Emily asked eagerly.

Actually, Pollard was in the city morgue, but Longarm wasn't ready to tell her that yet. Instead, he said, "I reckon he's still in Denver."

"What did he say? What did he tell you?"

Longarm hesitated, unsure of how much to reveal. He still didn't know what Emily Harrigan was really after.

Without waiting for him to answer, Emily rushed on, "Did he tell you where to find the gold?" She seemed genuinely excited now.

"What if he did?" Longarm asked, still being cagey.

"I hoped that my father had him tell you," Emily said. "I prayed that he would get word to you somehow! But I was afraid . . ." She sagged back in the chair, seeming to shrink a little. "I was afraid that he wouldn't. Father said he would never tell. I still held out some hope, though . . ."

Tears began to well from Emily's eyes and roll down her cheeks.

Longarm grimaced as he watched her take a lace handkerchief from her bag and wipe her eyes. Like most men, it nearly always bumfuzzled him when a woman started to cry. He was annoyed and uncomfortable and mostly felt like he ought to do *something*, but blamed if he knew what. He moved over to the edge of the bed and sat down on it so that he could look straight into Emily's face. As gently as he could, he said, "Maybe you'd better start at the first and tell me the whole thing, ma'am."

She dabbed at her eyes again with the hanky. "Yes, yes, you're right. You see, Marshal, my father was never really a bad man. He just . . . he just wound up on the wrong side of the law."

That was what most owlhoots wanted folks to believe, thought Longarm, but seldom was there any truth to it. Some men started riding the outlaw trail through no fault of their own, but they were few and far between. Most men who became outlaws did so because of greed, laziness, just plain cussedness, or all three.

He didn't say any of that to Emily Harrigan. He just waited for her to go on.

"I don't remember when I realized that he was . . . not a law-abiding man," she said. "I suppose it was when I was a young girl, when my mother was still alive. We lived in Santa Fe then. Father would be gone for weeks at a time, and I know now that was when he was off robbing banks and holding up trains. Then . . . then my mother passed away when I was fourteen. That was eight years ago. When my father got word, he came back to Santa Fe and took me from the neighbors who had been caring for me. He brought me here to Denver and we took a train for Philadelphia. Once we got there, he enrolled me in Miss Van Der Houton's Academy for Young Ladies."

Yep, thought Longarm, an even more highfalutin' name than usual for such a place.

"I knew my name was Emily Harrigan, but as far as the school was concerned, I was Emily Anderson. I figured out why when I saw newspaper stories about the Harrigan Gang. They became more notorious than ever once I was back east. I suppose Father thought he didn't have to worry about me anymore. He paid Miss Van Der Houton enough money so that he was confident I'd be

28

taken care of. When I graduated three years ago, Miss Van Der Houton asked me to remain at the school as an instructor. I wonder now if my father subsidized my salary."

Longarm ventured a question. "Did you know when he was captured and sent to prison?"

"Of course. It made the Philadelphia papers." Emily smiled faintly. "You may not know it, Marshal, but many people back east have an insatiable appetite for stories about the wild and wooly West."

Longarm knew it, all right, having encountered quite a few Eastern journalists and dime novelists during his career as a lawman.

Emily continued, "I tried to put him out of my mind. I had a life of my own to live, my post at the academy, an identity with no apparent connection to the infamous Clete Harrigan. I could have stayed there in Philadelphia."

"Why didn't you?" Longarm asked gently.

"Because . . . he's my father." Emily's voice twisted wretchedly. "Some people may be able to deny their own relatives and ignore the bonds of blood, Marshal Long, but I'm not one of them."

"What did you do? You said you went to Fort Leavenworth to see him?"

She nodded. "Several times, in fact. At first he was angry, but then I think he got to be glad to see me. He didn't like what I said to him, though. I tried to convince him that the best thing he could do for me and for himself and for everyone involved . . . was to reveal where he hid the money he stole in his last robbery. It was a large amount. A fortune, really."

"I know," Longarm said heavily. "I reckon your pa didn't cotton much to the idea?"

"He refused. I told him that he *had* to do it. He had to clear that stain on his conscience."

As far as Longarm was concerned, anybody who had

29

planned and pulled off as many robberies as Clete Harrigan had probably wasn't overly burdened with a conscience in the first place. Again, he kept those thoughts to himself. Instead, he asked, "Why was it so important to you?"

"Because it should have been important to him." Emily looked squarely into Longarm's eyes. "Because he's dying, Marshal Long, and he needs to make peace with himself and with the law before he goes."

Clete Harrigan—*dying?* That was news to Longarm. Of course, he thought as his eyes narrowed in surprise, he didn't keep tabs on the men he helped send to prison. And as a rule, hoosegows weren't very healthy places. Without trying to sound morbid about it, he asked, "What's wrong with him?"

"Consumption," Emily answered in a flat, bleak voice devoid of hope. "He didn't tell me about it at first. I suppose he wanted to keep it from me. But then his coughing got worse, and when I demanded to know what was causing it, he broke down and told me. I even talked to the prison doctor. There's . . . nothing anyone can do. Nothing."

Longarm felt sorry for her. Clete Harrigan might've been a lowdown skunk—no "might've" about it, Longarm thought—but he was still the gal's father. Clearly, she loved him whether he deserved that love or not. The pain she felt over his impending demise was real.

The news of Harrigan's illness finished tying things up as far as Longarm was concerned. It was time to come clean with Emily. She deserved that much.

"Floyd Pollard didn't tell me where that loot is stashed," Longarm said. "But he tried to."

Emily frowned a little and shook her head. "What do you mean, he tried to? Why couldn't he just tell you?"

"Because he'd been shot." Longarm delivered the news

30

bluntly. "He died before he could do anything except mention the gold."

Emily's eyes widened. One hand rose slowly to her mouth and clenched into a fist. "No," she said around it. "That can't be. Floyd . . . Floyd's dead?"

"I'm afraid so."

"But . . . but he was such a nice old man! Why would anyone want to hurt him?"

"Now, that I don't know," Longarm admitted. "Could be he ran into somebody who had a grudge against him from the time before he was in prison. Why was he sent to Leavenworth, anyway?"

"He was a civilian supplier for the army who embezzled money and defrauded the government. But he never really hurt anyone, at least not that I know of."

Longarm agreed that being a corrupt businessman didn't sound like the type of crime that would have men gunning for a fella years after the fact. A blood debt seemed unlikely.

Emily went on. "Could . . . could it have had something to do with the message my father sent to you?"

"That seems more likely. Pollard was already wounded when he showed up here. Before he could do more than say a few words, some hardcase finished him off with a shot from down the hall. I went after the gunman and a pard of his, and they tried to kill me, too."

"But you're here," Emily said. "You must have caught them. What did they say?"

Longarm could only shake his head. "They both wound up dead before I could ask them any questions. Sometimes when you land smack-dab in the middle of a corpse-and-cartridge session, there ain't no time to do anything except ventilate the other fellas the best you can before they ventilate you."

Emily paled, and Longarm thought that maybe he shouldn't have been quite so forthcoming about the details

31

of the ruckus. He went on hurriedly. "So I don't really know anything except that Pollard mentioned the stolen gold and said something about Sweetwater Canyon. Does that mean anything to you, Miss Harrigan?"

Longarm could see her turning the question over in her mind. "Sweetwater Canyon," she repeated in a musing tone. "It sounds familiar somehow, but . . . but I can't really recall. Is there such a place?"

"There's a Sweetwater City down in New Mexico Territory, right between the Sangre de Cristos and the San Luis Valley. My boss and I are thinking there might be a Sweetwater Canyon somewhere close by. That's why I'm going down there to have a look around." He drew his gold turnip from the watch pocket of his trousers and flipped open the case. "Fact is, I've got to go catch a train in just a little while."

Emily's face lit up with an idea. "Why don't I send a telegram to the prison and ask my father to tell me what he was going to have Floyd tell you? That way you'll know for sure about Sweetwater Canyon."

Longarm considered the suggestion. There might be time to send a wire to Leavenworth and get a reply before the southbound train pulled out. If he and Vail were completely off-trail with the Sweetwater Canyon idea, asking Harrigan about it directly might save a wasted trip.

"All right," he said with a nod. "That's a good idea. I'll go with you down to the telegraph office. It's on the way to the railroad station, anyway." He tossed his war-bag over his shoulder and picked up his saddle and the Winchester leaning in a corner of the room.

Emily came to her feet. He could tell she was still upset about Floyd Pollard's death, but an excited animation had returned to her blue eyes, replacing the despair that had been there earlier. Longarm could tell by that how important it was to her that the loot from her father's last job be recovered.

They went downstairs, Emily talking excitedly. "If Father was willing to send a message to you with Floyd, surely he'll tell me where to find that gold. I wish I had gone back to see him again. Obviously, what I said to him had an effect. He changed his mind about everything after my last visit."

Longarm was curious about something. As they left the boarding house and started along the street in the direction of the Western Union office and the railroad station, he said, "When you first told me who you are, you mentioned something about being grateful to me. What for, if you don't mind me asking?"

"Why, for arresting my father, of course. That brought his life of crime to an end before some lawman killed him."

Longarm didn't mention how close he had come to fatally wounding Harrigan during their gun battle. Nor did he venture the opinion that an old curly wolf like Clete Harrigan might well have preferred being dead to spending the rest of his life behind bars. Emily could think whatever she wanted to. As far as Longarm was concerned, the most important thing was finding the loot Harrigan had hidden—and bringing this whole business to a close at last.

Chapter 4

Before they could reach the telegraph office, Longarm spotted a familiar figure hurrying along the street toward them. Since the Federal Building was in that direction, too, he wasn't all that surprised to see Henry. The young man wore a bowler hat, and when he saw Longarm and Emily, he changed course slightly to intercept them.

"Looking for me, Henry?" Longarm asked when the young man came within earshot.

Henry nodded. "Yes, Chief Marshal Vail sent me out with a message for you." He glanced at Emily. Longarm could tell that Henry was curious about the young woman, but the big lawman didn't offer any explanations or introductions.

"Well, here I am, and I'm in sort of a hurry, so go ahead and take a bite out of the apple, old son."

"We got another wire from the prison at Fort Leavenworth," Henry said, turning his attention away from Emily and back to Longarm. "Clete Harrigan has taken a turn for the worse and is near death. He's not expected to regain consciousness."

Emily gasped in surprise and horror. Longarm's jaw tightened. He wished now he had taken the time to tell

Henry the identity of the young woman with him. Then maybe Henry wouldn't have blurted out the bad news in such a bald-faced way.

Henry blinked rapidly and stared uncomprehendingly at Emily. He knew he had done something wrong, but it was obvious he had no clue what it was.

Longarm set his saddle down, then put a hand on Emily's arm and squeezed gently. "I'm mighty sorry you had to hear it like that," he said. Glancing at Henry from the corner of his eyes, he added, "This is Miss Emily Harrigan. She's Clete Harrigan's daughter."

"Oh, my God!" Henry snatched the bowler hat off his head. "Miss Harrigan, I . . . I'm so sorry! I can't apologize enough for my . . . my rudeness and crudity and . . . and . . ."

Emily's eyes shone with tears again as she lifted a hand and said, "No, that's all right, sir. You couldn't have known." Her voice showed the strain she was under, but it still carried an undertone of strength.

"We were on our way to the telegraph office to send a wire to Leavenworth ourselves," Longarm explained to Henry. He didn't much like standing around on the street discussing the case with the youngster, but there was no other choice. He had to count on Henry to take the news back to Billy Vail. There was no time for anything else before the southbound train pulled out. Even going to the Western Union office would have been cutting it close.

Now it appeared that there was no reason to stop and send a wire. Clete Harrigan was in no shape to answer it.

Quickly, Longarm told Henry about Harrigan's decision, prompted by Emily's visits to him in prison, to reveal where he had cached the loot from his gang's last robbery. "That must be why Pollard showed up on my doorstep. He was passing along what Harrigan told him to tell me."

"But . . . but who shot him?" Henry asked in confusion.

35

Longarm didn't have an answer for that. "Maybe I'll find out when I get to Sweetwater Canyon." He glanced at Emily and lowered his voice as he went on, "Reckon I'll be heading straight for the depot now."

"Excuse me," Emily said. "Why did the prison send another telegram about my father to Marshal Vail?"

"This wire came directly from the prison doctor," Henry said, eager to be helpful and make amends for his painfully blunt revelation. "He noticed the message we sent asking about Pollard, and he thought we'd like to know about Harrigan's condition, too. I mean, about your father's condition, Miss Harrigan. Again, I apologize—"

Longarm didn't have time to stand around all day listening to Henry apologize. He broke in, "Why don't you take Miss Harrigan to see Marshal Vail, Henry? I reckon he'll want to hear the whole story from her, what we know of it, anyway."

"Oh, no," Emily said before Henry had a chance to reply. "I'm going with you, Marshal Long."

Now it was Longarm's turn to be thunderstruck. "Ma'am?" he got out after a moment. "Going where with me?"

"Why, to help you find Sweetwater Canyon, of course."

Longarm resisted the temptation to take off his hat, scratch his head, and scrub a hand over his face in frustration. Ever since that pounding on his door the night before had ruined what should have been a mighty nice evening, this case had been taking unexpected twists and turns, like a rattlesnake sidewinding through the dirt. And each new twist brought more unanswered questions, so that he felt like he never could quite get a handle on things.

He was certain of this much, though—he was going to Sweetwater Canyon, and he didn't want any company on the trip, no matter how blond and blue-eyed and pretty that company might be.

"I don't reckon that's a good idea," he said with a shake of his head. "You don't know what you're suggesting, Miss Harrigan."

"Of course I do," Emily insisted. "I told you, I spent a lot of my childhood in New Mexico Territory, Marshal. I can help you—"

Longarm broke in dryly, "No offense, miss, but I've ridden over most of that territory more'n once. I can find my way around."

"You didn't know where Sweetwater City was," Emily pointed out.

Longarm's jaw tightened. "I don't reckon I've been to every little settlement and wide spot in the trail. I still don't need no civilian tagging along with me, especially a gal." Emily's feelings might be hurt by the bluntness of his statement, but he couldn't help that.

"I can take care of myself. I was raised on the frontier."

"Miss Van Der Houton's Academy for Young Ladies is a mighty long way from the frontier."

Emily glared at him. Longarm saw the stubborn set of her jaw and knew that she was a young woman who was accustomed to getting her way, at least part of the time. Losing her mother like she had, and having her father dump her in some school hundreds of miles away from him, must have toughened her. He had seen some strong-willed headmistresses in such schools. Miss Van Der Houton had passed some of that along to Emily Harrigan.

But where he was going, chances were there would be trouble. What had happened to Floyd Pollard was proof of that. The more Longarm thought about it, the more convinced he was that the two hardcases had gunned Pollard because they hadn't wanted him talking to Longarm. Somehow, the gunmen had known about the message Pollard was carrying from Clete Harrigan. If they didn't want Pollard telling Longarm where to find the stolen gold, that had to mean they were after it themselves.

37

Them . . . or the person they had been working for. The two killers were dead, but the coins in their pockets indicated that someone had paid them to dispose of the old man. That person, whoever it was, was still alive, still out there somewhere.

And when Longarm headed for New Mexico, the man or woman who had paid the gunmen to kill Pollard likely would guess that the big lawman was on the trail of the loot. It would be a race for the gold between Longarm and however many owlhoots were also after the hidden loot.

All those thoughts clicked together in his mind. He was sure the theory was correct. He put a hand on Emily's arm again and went on, "Henry, escort the young lady back to the Federal Building. After she's talked to Marshal Vail, see that she gets a room in a decent hotel."

"Wait just a minute!" Emily said angrily. "You have no right to tell me where I can and can't go, Marshal."

Longarm's voice was deliberately cool as he replied, "I reckon I do. I'm a federal lawman on a job for Uncle Sam, and it'd be a dereliction of duty for me to drag you along with me, Miss Harrigan."

"But . . . but . . ." She was sputtering now as Longarm gently pushed her toward Henry. For his part, Henry looked like he rather would have been saddled with a wildcat than have to take charge of Emily Harrigan. He had to know, though, that Longarm was right about not letting her go along.

Carefully, Henry reached out toward her. "Ah, Miss Harrigan, if you would, ah, come with me . . ." he began. He took her other arm.

Emily pulled away from both of them. "Aren't you two a fine pair of big strong lawmen?" she asked, her voice dripping with scorn. "Does it take both of you to handle one girl? Or manhandle one girl, I should say!"

Henry glanced around the street, clearly embarrassed

that Emily was making a scene. Longarm didn't have time to be embarrassed. He gave Henry a curt nod and said, "I'll see you when I get back." He picked up his saddle and strode away, letting his long legs carry him at a faster pace now. Behind him, he heard Henry talking rapidly and worriedly as he tried to convince Emily to come with him to Billy Vail's office.

Longarm didn't look back. He had enough to think about without seeing the anger and disappointment and grief that he knew he would see if he looked in Emily Harrigan's eyes.

The Union Pacific ran south from Denver to the town of Pueblo, on the Arkansas River, before curving southeastward across the Texas Panhandle to Fort Worth. The train carrying Longarm pulled into Pueblo late that afternoon. From here he could catch a stagecoach that would follow the road south through Raton Pass to the settlement of Raton, where he had captured Clete Harrigan in the first place. From there he could rent a horse, cut west through the mountains, and eventually come to Sweetwater City. He hoped the ride wouldn't take more than a few days.

He stepped off the train onto the platform at the Pueblo station and looked around with his customary caution. If his speculations about the killing of Floyd Pollard and everything it meant were correct, there might be an attempt made to stop him from reaching his goal. Not only that, but he had made plenty of enemies in his career. He always kept his eyes open and watched his back trail. That was one way of staying alive.

Nobody seemed to be paying any attention to him. He carried his warbag, saddle, and Winchester over to the ticket window and asked the clerk if the stagecoach station was in the same place it had been the last time he was in Pueblo. Having been assured that it was, Longarm left the depot and walked down the street in the fading light. The sun was about to dip behind the mountain peaks to the west.

Luck was with him. According to the schedule chalked on a board next to the door of the stage line office, the next coach for Raton would be pulling out in less than an hour, right after supper. The Concord coach, painted red with yellow trim, was parked in front of the cavernous barn next to the office building. The team that had brought it here had been unhitched, and soon the hostlers would lead out six fresh horses.

Longarm stepped up to the ticket window built into the front of the building and said to the man inside, "I need to get to Raton. Does the stage lay over between here and there or keep rolling all night?"

"Lay over in Trinidad," the ticket agent replied, naming a town just north of the border between Colorado and New Mexico Territory. Raton Pass was a short distance south of Trinidad, and the town of Raton was at the bottom of the pass. Once the stage pulled out of Trinidad in the morning, it would take only an hour or so to reach Raton. Longarm felt a twinge of impatience. If the stage was going as far south as Trinidad tonight, why didn't it just go on to Raton?

He knew the answer, of course. The jehu would want good light before he attempted to drive the stagecoach down the steep, treacherous road through the pass. Longarm couldn't really blame him for that.

"One ticket," Longarm said, and when the transaction was concluded, he asked, "Where's the best place to get something to eat around here?"

The agent jerked a thumb over his shoulder. "Come on in. The dining room here at the station is as cheap as anywhere, and the grub ain't too bad."

Longarm nodded. "Much obliged. Can I leave my gear out here until the stage is ready to load?"

"Hell, the boot's open. Go ahead and chuck your bag

and saddle in there. The hostlers'll keep an eye on them. Imagine you want to keep that long gun with you."

Longarm nodded again and tucked the Winchester under his arm. He stowed his gear in the coach's rear boot, then stepped over to the door and went into the station.

The dining room was to his left. He had barely stepped into the room when a voice called, "Howlin' horned toads! If it ain't Custis Long!"

Longarm winced, both at the scratchy voice and the fact that his identity had just been announced to everyone in the dining room. If he had any enemies here, they had just been alerted to his presence. He summoned up a grin for the short, stocky man who stood up from the long trestle table and came over to him, hand outstretched.

The man was in his fifties, with long white hair and a bristly beard. His eyes were bright under bushy white eyebrows. He wore a long duster over range clothes. As he shook hands with Longarm, he went on, "Good to see you again, son. How long's it been?"

"A couple of years, at least."

The old-timer snorted. "More like seven or eight. 'Twas over on the Canadian River, I recollect, 'round about the time the buffler herds started dwindlin' down so much it weren't worth the time an' trouble to hunt 'em no more. You was one o' the shooters, and I drove the hide wagon."

Longarm nodded, remembering his brief stint as a buffalo hunter. He hadn't cared for it, and he had gone back to cowboying after only a short time at the job. And not long after that, he had pinned on a lawman's badge for the first time.

"How are you, Cougar?"

"Oh, I'm fine, I reckon. You see that purty stagecoach outside?"

"I sure did," Longarm said.

"I'm drivin' it now," Cougar Powell said, his chest puffing out with pride. "Come up in the world, I reckon I

41

have. From drivin' a hide wagon to bein' the jehu on a stagecoach. Coach don't stink near as bad as the hide wagon, neither . . . most o' the time." Cougar frowned and cast a glance over his shoulder at the passengers seated at the table. Clearly, he wasn't all that fond of some of them.

Quickly, Longarm looked them over as well, since he was going to be traveling with them tonight and in the morning. A couple of men wore bright plaid suits and had derbies on the table next to them. Drummers of some sort, thought Longarm. The other two men were narrow-faced and hard-eyed and just looking at them rang warning bells in the back of Longarm's mind. Chances were the men were just drifting cowhands, but they also had the look of Coltmen about them, like the two Longarm had been forced to kill up in Denver less than twenty-four hours earlier.

Cougar slapped Longarm on the shoulder. "What are you doin' these days, boy? Can't be huntin' buffler no more. Them days is gone."

So the old-timer didn't know that he had become a lawman. That was good, Longarm decided. The leather folder containing his badge and bona fides was tucked away in his pocket. He didn't intend to advertise the fact that he was a star packer. Maybe those two hardcases didn't know who he was. They were a making a point of concentrating on their stew and cornbread, rather than paying any attention to him and Cougar. Of course, that could be an act to make him think he wasn't in any danger.

"I did some cowboying," Longarm replied honestly. "Drifted around a lot." That was true, too; it was just that his travels usually came in the course of doing his job for the Justice Department. He shrugged. Let Cougar draw his own conclusions.

"You ridin' with me?"

"As far as Raton."

"Well, if you got the fare, I'm mighty glad to have you along. Maybe you'd like to ride up top with me so's we can chew the fat 'bout the old days."

"We'll see," Longarm said without promising anything. Under normal circumstances, he would have enjoyed spending the next few hours atop the coach with Cougar. He would do a lot more listening than he would talking, but that was all right. He would make a better target on top of the coach, though, if anybody wanted to take a potshot at him.

With night coming on, that was unlikely. He didn't relish the idea of sitting inside the coach with two possible gunmen, either. Maybe he would take Cougar up on that offer. For now, he wanted to get something to eat.

"Sit down," Cougar said as if reading his mind. "Get yourself on the outside of a surroundin.' "

A middle-aged woman in a shapeless dress came out of the kitchen with a bowl. She set it in front of Longarm and filled it with stew from the pot in the center of the table. She gave him a plate of cornbread as well, and Longarm dug in gratefully. He'd eaten an apple on the train from Denver, but that was all the food he'd had since breakfast.

As the woman went back in the kitchen, Cougar sat down beside Longarm and nudged him in the side with an elbow. "You see her, Custis? Her an' me are sweethearts."

Longarm grinned. "You thinking about settling down, Cougar?"

The old man cackled. "Hell, no! She don't know 'bout all the sweethearts I got in ever' other settlement along the blamed stage line!"

Longarm ate quickly so that he could finish the meal at the same time as the others. He didn't want to delay the stage. Cougar put on a battered old hat with a pushed-

up brim and went out to see that the fresh team was hitched up to his liking. Longarm hadn't spoken to the other passengers, but he gave the two drummers a polite nod. The other two men still seemed to be ignoring him. They pushed back from the table and went outside, causing Longarm to frown slightly. If he'd had his druthers, he would have liked to get outside before the two hardcases. Stepping from a lighted room into darkness could be dangerous if somebody who wanted to kill you was lurking in the shadows.

The stage would be leaving soon, though, and he couldn't stay here. He stood up, pushed aside the empty bowl and plate, dropped a coin beside them to pay for the meal, and turned toward the door. Behind him, the two drummers talked and laughed in low tones. Probably they were friends. Traveling salesmen got to know and like each other out here on the frontier, except for the ones who were really cutthroat about their business.

Longarm was almost at the door when a voice said behind him, "All right, Long, that's far enough. Stand right there and put up your hands."

The unmistakable sound of two guns being cocked punctuated the order.

Chapter 5

Longarm froze. His teeth clenched together and he grated a heartfelt curse. He had recognized the voice that ordered him to stop and put his hands up. It belonged to one of the drummers.

A muffled exclamation of surprise sounded, and one of the men said, "Damn it, Bennie, grab her!"

For just a second, a woman screamed. But then the sound was cut off short, too quickly for it to have been heard outside, and Longarm knew one of the drummers had clapped a hand over the mouth of the waitress. She must have stepped into the dining room from the kitchen at just the wrong moment, taking the would-be killers by surprise.

And Longarm had no doubt the men intended to kill him. Their deceptive appearance had fooled him. Both drummers had seemed soft, mild, no threat at all. The voice that barked the orders, though, was flint-hard, the sort of voice that belonged to a man who wouldn't hesitate to shoot to kill.

"Your hands ain't up, Long," the man said now.

Slowly, Longarm raised his arms. The phony salesmen probably didn't want to kill him right here in the middle of the stage station dining room, with Pueblo's busy main street right outside. They would take him out the back of the building at gunpoint, maybe knock him unconscious and dispose of him elsewhere. But if pushed to it, he had no doubt they would gun him down where he stood. They were probably being well paid to get rid of him and were willing to take a chance or two for their blood money.

"Slide back here toward us," the spokesman went on, confirming Longarm's guess about what they intended to do.

His own voice hard as stone, Longarm said, "Maybe you better just go ahead and do what you came to do, old son." It was unlikely he would be able to spin around, draw his Colt, and get a shot off before he took a bullet or two, but he figured he would live long enough to at least have a chance of sending the bastards to hell ahead of him.

"Take it easy, Long," the boss gunman said with a chuckle. "If you don't cooperate, I'll just have Bennie cut this woman's throat, nice and quiet-like."

Longarm's nerves grew even more taut. The waitress blundering in had made things worse. By threatening her, they could make Longarm do whatever they wanted, because he couldn't stand by and just let them murder her.

"That old stage driver's gonna be coming back in here to see what's holding us up," Longarm said, stalling for time.

"Not for a few minutes yet. He's still on schedule. And by the time he does, we'll all be out of here. There are horses waiting for us in the trees out back."

So the attempt had been well planned, thought Longarm. His enemies had moved quickly. They must have been watching him and had seen him leave Denver on the train. They had gotten ahead of him somehow, probably on fast horses. The train hadn't been an express; it had made stops at Colorado Springs, Castle Rock, and several

other towns on the way down here. The gunmen might have ridden their horses to death getting to Pueblo faster than the railroad, but it could be done.

"Come on, come on," the boss drummer said, getting impatient now. His time was running out.

Longarm took a step back. He was going to have to go along with them for now and hope that he got a chance to turn the tables on them.

"That's far enough!"

The voice came from the back of the room, and once again Longarm was taken by surprise. If he hadn't known better, he would have sworn that it belonged to Emily Harrigan.

"There's a greener pointed right at you," the woman's voice went on. "One more step and I'll blow you in half! Now let go of that woman and drop your guns!"

Longarm couldn't stand it any longer. He had to turn and look.

Emily was there, all right, just inside the rear door of the station, and she had a shotgun in her hands. Both barrels were cocked as she trained the weapon on the two drummers. The barrels trembled a little, but that was probably due to the weight of the scattergun, not to any nerves on Emily's part. Her face was calm, her eyes steady.

"Marshal Long, are you all right?" she called to him.

Longarm finished turning around and reached for his Colt as he said, "I reckon." He wasn't going to question his good fortune, not until he had both of the phony drummers disarmed and in custody. Then he would take the time to ask Emily how the hell she had just happened to show up here in Pueblo when she was supposed to be back in Denver.

"I told you to let her go," Emily snapped at the phony drummer who was still holding the waitress.

Suddenly, the man twisted around and shoved the woman straight toward Emily. Emily gasped and jerked

47

the barrels of the shotgun toward the ceiling. With that threat removed, the drummer jerked up his gun and fired past the waitress at Emily. The bullet missed and knocked splinters from the doorjamb behind her.

The gunman got off only one shot. Longarm's revolver bucked in his hand as it roared. The bullet smashed into the drummer's back and threw him forward.

The other man, the one who'd been giving the orders, had his weapon drawn and ready. He fired at Longarm. The bullet burned past the lawman's ear. In the confusion, Longarm caught a glimpse of Emily shoving the waitress out of the line of fire. Then the shotgun erupted with a sound like thunder.

The second drummer pitched forward, blood flying from his mouth. His feet went out from under him and he belly-flopped, landing face down on the rough wooden floor of the stage station. His back was an ugly sight, the double charge of buckshot having struck him there at close range. Emily had threatened to blow him in half, and she had damned near done it.

Longarm stood there tensely for a second, gun leveled in case either of the phony drummers was still alive. Neither man moved, however. Longarm stepped forward, kicked the guns they had dropped well out of reach. Then he looked at Emily. Her face was white as milk, and her eyes were so big he could see white all around their blue centers. Then those eyes rolled up in her head, the shotgun slipped from suddenly nerveless fingers, and she swayed and collapsed in a dead faint.

The front door of the station slammed open. Cougar Powell and the ticket agent rushed in, each of them holding a gun in his hand. The hostlers from the barn were right behind them, armed with the sharp-tined forks they used to pitch hay. The men all came to a stop and stared at the bloody shapes sprawled on the floor.

"By the great horn spoon!" Cougar yelled. "What in blazes happened?"

Longarm gestured with the barrel of his gun toward the dead drummers. "Haul these carcasses out of here," he ordered. He holstered his Colt and went over to the waitress, who stood with her hands over her face, shaking with fear. "It's all right, ma'am," Longarm told her. "Those fellas won't hurt you. They won't hurt anybody again."

The woman lowered her hands, spotted the bushy-bearded jehu on the other side of the room, and wailed, "Cougar!" She rushed over to him and threw herself in his arms. He staggered a little under the impact but kept his feet, patting the woman on the back in an attempt to calm her as he stared over her shoulder at Longarm and looked mighty confused.

Longarm knelt beside Emily and carefully lifted her into a sitting position. Bracing her against his body, he slapped her face lightly and said, "Emily! Emily, wake up!"

Her eyelids fluttered open a moment later, revealing the wide blue orbs. "Oh!" she gasped. "Oh, my goodness! Did I . . . did I really shoot . . . oh, my!"

Longarm chuckled. "You saved my bacon, that's what you did. Come on, let's get you up to the table."

He helped her onto the bench next to the table. A glance over his shoulder told him that the hostlers had dragged out the corpses of the two drummers, as he had ordered, so at least Emily was spared that gruesome sight. There were still several puddles of blood on the floor, though, and Longarm saw her looking at them. A shudder went through her. He felt it as he sat there with his arm around her shoulders.

"It's all right," he told her. "It's all over."

"I shot them, didn't I?" she asked, her voice dull, stunned by what had happened. "I really shot them."

"Well, truth be told, you only ventilated one of the

49

buzzards. I did for the other one. But they're both dead, sure enough."

Cougar managed to get the weeping waitress into the arms of the ticket agent. Looking relieved, he came over to the table and said, "Lord Almighty, Custis. What the hell's goin' on here? When this little lady come runnin' up and said you was in trouble, I didn't believe her at first. But when she grabbed my ol' greener and took off 'round the buildin', I knew somethin' was wrong."

"I . . . I saw them through the window when I came up to the station," Emily said. Her voice was a little stronger now, and a bit of color had seeped back into her face. "I knew I had to do something to help you, Marshal Long. I saw them pointing guns at you and assaulting that poor woman."

"Reckon you saved our lives," Longarm said. "It was a mite dangerous, though, going up against two gunmen like that."

"I might not have been brave enough to do it . . . if I'd stopped to think about it."

Longarm smiled faintly. That was the way it happened a lot of times, he thought. Most heroic actions would never be carried out if people just stopped to think about what they were doing.

A stocky man with a big hat and sweeping gray mustaches came into the room and clumped over to the table, the spurs on his boots jingling. He had a star pinned to his vest. "What the hell happened here?" he demanded harshly. "I got two dead men outside, both of them shot in the back."

Longarm got to his feet. "Maybe so, Sheriff," he said, "but front or back, killing those jaspers was self-defense, pure and simple."

The local lawman was a head shorter than Longarm. He peered up pugnaciously at the federal deputy and said, "Is that so? And just who would you be, mister?"

50

There was no point in keeping his identity a secret, Longarm decided. The men he was up against already knew who he was. "I'm Deputy U.S. Marshal Custis Long," he told the sheriff. "Hang on a minute, and I'll show you my badge and bona fides." He reached for the leather folder.

The sheriff rested his hand on the walnut butt of an old Colt revolver. "Take it slow and easy," he advised.

Longarm carefully withdrew his identification. After looking at the badge and documents for a few seconds, the sheriff grunted and handed them back over. "So you're a federal man," he said. "That still don't explain those killin's."

Longarm did so as succinctly as possible. Cougar brought the waitress over, and she backed up Longarm's story, telling the sheriff that if not for Longarm and Emily, the two phony drummers would have killed her.

"Sounds like a straight story," the sheriff admitted. "Why'd those two ol' boys want to kill you, Long?"

"That's a story its ownself," Longarm said, "only it ain't straight and it ain't short. The upshot of it is that they were trying to keep me from getting to a place down in New Mexico Territory called Sweetwater City."

"Think I've heard of it, but I ain't sure. Hired killers, were they?"

"That's what I figure. It'd be a good idea to have a look through their pockets."

The sheriff crooked his hand. "Come on with me, then. I had 'em taken down to the undertaker's place."

Longarm turned to Cougar. "Can you keep an eye on Miss Harrigan for me?"

"Sure thing ... though the way she handled that greener o' mine, I ain't sure she needs anybody to look after her."

Longarm thought Emily still looked pretty shaken by

51

the events of the past quarter-hour. He said to Cougar, "Stay with her anyway."

"Will do." The old-timer paused and added, "You could've told me you was a lawdog, though, Custis. I wouldn't't've held it against you . . . too much."

Longarm grinned and followed the sheriff out of the stage station.

The local lawman's name was Albie Sutton. He introduced himself to Longarm as they walked down the street to Pueblo's undertaking parlor. "Seems like I've heard of you, Marshal," Sutton mused. "Ain't you the one they call Longarm?"

"Sometimes. My friends generally call me Custis."

"You got any idea why those fellas wanted to plug you? Or was it just on general principles?"

Longarm grinned. "Could be they had a grudge against me for something that happened in the past. I reckon it's more likely they're tied in with the job that's taking me to New Mexico. I'll have a better notion once we've gone through their pockets. This undertaker of yours, is he honest?"

"Honest as the day is long. Why do you ask?"

"Because there's a fair chance we'll find a good number of double eagles on those carcasses."

A few minutes later, that turned out to be exactly right. Each of the two dead men had been carrying over a hundred dollars in gold pieces. Sheriff Sutton hefted the coins in his hand and frowned. "Anybody goin' to put in a claim on this money?"

"Not likely," Longarm said.

"Some of it'll go to pay for puttin' these jaspers in the ground, then, and the rest into the county coffers. You never saw 'em before?"

Longarm shook his head. "Nope." For the second night in a row, total strangers had tried to kill him. That was getting tiresome.

Now that he took a closer look at them, he could see the owlhoot stripe in them. The gaudy suits and the derbies had fooled him into thinking they were harmless. The trick had almost worked. It might have if Emily Harrigan hadn't come barging in with that scattergun, Longarm thought grimly.

Reminded of Emily, he said to Sutton, "Sheriff, if you don't need anything else from me, I want to get back to the stage station. I reckon ol' Cougar will be pulling out for Trinidad pretty soon, and I don't want to miss the stage."

"You ain't goin' to tell me exactly what it is you're about, are you?"

"Federal business," Longarm said. "Once I'm gone from here, though, you shouldn't have any more trouble."

Sutton grunted. "Go on, then. I've got your statement. That'll do for the inquest, such as it is."

Longarm left the lawman at the undertaking parlor and walked quickly back to the stage station. He wanted to check on Emily, too, before the stage left. Even though he was grateful for what she had done, he had a few questions for her . . . such as what in blue blazes she was doing in Pueblo.

He found her sitting at the table in the station with Cougar, drinking coffee and looking much better than when he had left. Cougar nodded to Longarm and went out to the coach. Emily summoned up a smile for Longarm as he sat down next to her. "Hello, Marshal."

"Where'd you learn to handle a greener like that?" he asked without returning the greeting. He didn't feel in an overly polite mood.

A faint smile tugged at the corners of Emily's mouth. "I told you, I was raised in the West. No amount of time spent in Philadelphia can change that."

"Well, I'm much obliged for what you did," he admitted. "I'd like to know, though, what you're doing here. I told Henry to take you to see Marshal Vail, then check you into a hotel."

She smiled again. "Poor Henry. He got so flustered when I told him I was having *lady problems* while we were on our way to the Federal Building that I didn't have any trouble at all slipping away from him."

Longarm couldn't help himself. He burst out laughing as he thought about Henry trying to cope with such a thing. "I reckon as soon as you gave him the slip you hightailed it down to the train station?"

"That's right. I barely made it in time. I was careful not to ride in the same car as you on the trip down."

"And then you followed me here to the stage station?"

Emily sipped her coffee. "And you know the rest."

Longarm looked at her for a long moment, then sighed and shook his head. "Bound and determined to go with me to New Mexico, aren't you?"

"I told you, I want to help you." Emily put her cup aside and turned halfway around on the bench, leaning forward slightly as her eyes searched his face. "I want to help you, Marshal. Like I told you, my father wasn't always around when I was a little girl, but I still know him better than you do. I can help you find where he hid that stolen gold."

Longarm wasn't sure Emily knew her father as well as she thought she did. Maybe she never had. And several years in prison could have changed Clete Harrigan even more.

"You've seen for yourself how somebody's trying to stop me from getting to Sweetwater Canyon," he pointed out. "It's going to be dangerous every step of the way."

"I'm willing to take that chance," she declared.

"You ain't the one responsible, though. I'm a lawman. It's my job to look out for folks and keep them safe."

"If you try to make me stay here or send me back to Denver, I'll just come after you anyway," Emily said, her

54

eyes bright with defiance once again. "How safe will that be?"

She had a point. If she was with him, at least he could keep an eye on her. He didn't want to admit that, though. He made one more try to convince her of the idea's folly.

"There's no stage line from Raton over the mountains. We'd have to travel by horseback."

A grin lit up Emily's face. "I rode every week at a stable in Philadelphia. All the girls from the academy did."

"Crossing the Sangre de Cristos in a hull on the back of a half-wild mustang is a mite different from trotting around some big city park."

"Give me a chance, Marshal. I won't hold you back."

Despite his misgivings, Longarm had a feeling she was right. Having her along might even come in handy. She sure enough had been handy when she showed up with that greener.

"All right," he said.

He thought she was trying not to look too pleased with herself as she smiled and picked up her coffee cup. "Thank you."

Cougar Powell came in a moment later. "You still goin' to Raton with me, Custis?"

Longarm got to his feet. "Yes, and so is Miss Harrigan."

"Well, come on, then," Cougar said with a wave of his hand. "We done wasted enough time here tonight. Behind schedule already, dang it."

Longarm took Emily's arm and went outside with her, the two of them following the old jehu. Emily had only one bag, something of a rarity where females were concerned, thought Longarm. He picked it up and stashed it in the boot for her, then opened the door of the stagecoach.

As he helped her in, something occurred to him. He

looked up at the driver's box, where Cougar was settling himself on the seat. "Where are those other two passengers?"

"Them two mean-lookin' fellers?" Cougar looked down at Longarm and shook his head. "They up an' disappeared after all the ruckus broke out. Don't know where they went, but I reckon they decided they didn't want to go to Raton after all."

Longarm frowned as his grip on the door tightened. He had a feeling he knew what had happened to the two men. His instincts about them had been right. They had been sent by his mysterious adversary, but they hadn't been the shooters. The two phony drummers had been given that chore. The other two were just there to watch and report.

But Longarm had no doubt that right now they were on their way back to wherever they had come from, to warn their boss that he was still alive—and still a danger to someone's plans.

Chapter 6

The rocking motion of a stagecoach could either lull a person to sleep or shake the teeth right out of his head, depending on the surface of the road and the skill of the driver. The road from Pueblo to Trinidad was fairly good, and Cougar Powell had years of experience at handling a team. So the ride wasn't too bad inside the coach for Longarm and Emily. They were the only passengers. With a gap-toothed grin, Cougar had commented that under the circumstances he didn't blame Longarm for choosing to ride inside with a pretty gal rather than up top with a grizzled old codger like him.

As the coach rocked and swayed on the broad leather thoroughbraces that supported it, Longarm and Emily talked about the case that had drawn them together. He tried to pick her brain about her outlaw father without being too obvious about it, but nothing she could remember seemed like a probable clue to where Harrigan might have hidden that loot. Gradually, their conversation diminished. They were sitting side by side in the coach's rear seat, facing forward, and after a few minutes of companionable silence, Longarm felt Emily slide over against him. Her head nudged his shoulder. He realized she was dozing off. The long day had finally caught up to her.

Longarm smiled as Emily snuggled against him with a sigh and settled deeper into sleep. It was dark in the coach; a couple of lighted lanterns hung on hooks on the outside of the vehicle, but there were no lights inside. Her body was warm and soft against him, and he could smell the pleasant scent of the perfume she wore, with the even more pleasant scent of female flesh underlying it. He stretched his long legs out in front of him and crossed them at the ankles. If he just had a cheroot going now, he would have been utterly content, but he figured it might disturb her if he lit a smoke. He was satisfied enough with the way things were. Hell, he thought drowsily, nobody was shooting at him. That was a definite improvement.

Somewhere along the way, he dozed off as well. He wasn't sure how long he slept. Probably not very long. The coach was still rolling along briskly when he roused from slumber. Something had woken him, but he wasn't sure what it was.

Then he realized that Emily's hand was resting on his crotch, and his shaft had hardened into a considerable lump right under her palm.

Longarm stiffened all over in surprise. Emily stirred a little and murmured something, then settled against him again. He listened to her deep, regular breathing and knew she was still asleep.

So the way she was touching him was just an accident, he told himself. She had shifted around in her sleep, and her hand had just happened to drop onto that portion of his anatomy. Well, he thought, accidents happen. It was nothing to worry about. He could just sit there and enjoy the intimacy.

On the other hand, if Emily woke up and found herself groping him like she was some sort of soiled dove, she would be mighty embarrassed, Longarm figured. He liked to think that he was a gentleman, despite his rough exterior. If he could do something to save Emily from some embarrassment, it was his duty to do so. He tried sliding his hips over a little on the seat, in hopes that her hand would drop down alongside his leg.

That didn't work. Her hand stayed where it was, and now that his body was at a slightly different angle, the upper part was pressed even closer to her. He felt the sweet softness of her breast prodding the side of his chest.

Emily made sleepy sounds again. If he wasn't careful, Longarm told himself, he was going to wake her, and then all his good intentions would be ruined. Of course, the road to Hades was paved with good intentions, he reminded himself, at least according to the old saying.

There was nothing hellish about what Emily was doing to him. In fact, it felt mighty good. The rocking motion of the coach made her hand move a little from time to time. The long, thick pole of male flesh inside Longarm's trousers responded to the involuntary stroking. He was so aroused that it was becoming painful. But there was no way he could reach down and unfasten his buttons so that he could get a little relief. That would wake up Emily for sure.

And to think he had worried that lighting a cheroot might disturb her!

The thought almost made him laugh out loud, but he held back the laughter. This was serious business. Emily was a graduate of Miss Van Der Houton's Academy for Young Ladies. What would Miss Van Der Houton think if she saw one of her pupils rubbing the talleywhacker of some rough-hewn frontier lawman? She'd be scandalized, that's what. Longarm gritted his teeth. His shoulders shook as he struggled to suppress another laugh. Damn it, he thought, how could anything be so funny and so arousing at the same blasted time?

He had to move her hand himself; that was all there was to it. That might wake her, but at least then he could

59

claim he was just trying to hold her hand. He reached down and slowly started trying to slide his fingers underneath hers.

Reflexes made her hand jump away from his, but then it came back down in the same place. Her fingers curled, gripping him through the fabric of his trousers. Good Lord! thought Longarm. She really was groping him now. He'd just made things worse.

The coach hit a bump and swayed up and down. Emily's grasp never loosened, but the pumping motion of her hand made things even more uncomfortable for Longarm. He wasn't having to fight off laughter any more. Things were getting serious.

There was nothing left for him to do. He had to get her hand out of his lap. He took a deep breath, reached down, and grabbed it, snatching it up and away from his privates as fast as he could. Emily came awake with a startled "Oh!" She straightened on the seat and looked around wildly. "What . . . where are we? Marshal Long? What are you doing?"

Longarm realized he still had hold of her hand, was gripping it a mite tightly, in fact. He was about to say something—although he wasn't sure just what it was going to be—when the coach lurched again and started slowing down. "Trinidad!" Cougar Powell yelled back from the driver's seat. "Comin' into Trinidad!"

A relieved grin spread over Longarm's face. "Sorry, Miss Harrigan," he said. "Didn't mean to startle you. I was waking you up to let you know we were here."

"Oh," Emily said again. "I . . . I understand." She paused, then went on, "Marshal, did I . . . did I go to *sleep* on you?"

"You dozed off a mite," Longarm said diplomatically.

"I'm so sorry. I didn't mean to—"

"That's all right," Longarm broke in. "Don't worry

about it. I got a little drowsy myself. Riding in a stage-coach at night will do that."

He'd had a close call, Longarm told himself. But things had worked out without anyone having to be overly embarrassed.

Now if that blasted tree trunk in his pants would just go down . . .

The coach rocked to a stop a few moments later. Longarm waited for the dust swirling around it to settle, then opened the door and stepped out. He turned back to help Emily down.

The hour was late, probably close to midnight. The office of the Trinidad stage station was dark, but there was a lantern burning in the barn and a couple of sleepy-eyed hostlers came out to unhitch the team. Longarm looked along the street and saw that most of the businesses were closed for the night. Up at the other end of the street, lights and the faint sound of a tinkling piano marked the location of the local saloons, which were still doing a brisk trade. Longarm recalled from his last visit to the town that there was a hotel a couple of blocks away.

He took Emily's arm and said to Cougar, "Miss Harrigan and I will go get rooms for the night."

"Suit yourselves," the jehu replied. "I plan on bunkin' in the loft. We'll be rollin' out of here in the mornin' at eight o'clock."

"We'll be ready," Longarm promised.

He and Emily walked along the street toward the hotel. Longarm's eyes darted here and there, alert for any sign of an ambush. He frowned at the dark mouth of an alley as they passed it, but nothing happened. No gun flame lanced from the shadows.

Whoever was out to stop him, it might take them a while to set up another trap for him. The fact that they had gone to so much trouble already was proof positive in Longarm's mind that he was on the right trail. That

61

loot of Harrigan's had to be stashed in Sweetwater Canyon, and he was more convinced than ever that the canyon itself was down near Sweetwater City.

A few more days and they would have the answer, he promised himself—if they could manage to live that long.

A balding, middle-aged clerk dozed behind the desk in the hotel lobby. He came awake with a gasp as Longarm and Emily walked in. Blinking rapidly, he licked his lips and then said, "Ah, good evening, folks. Welcome to Trinidad." Without looking back, he reached behind him and plucked a key from a nail on the board. "Got a fine room for you. Just sign the register . . ."

"Two rooms," Longarm said.

The clerk blinked again. "Excuse me?"

"Two rooms," Longarm repeated. "One for the young lady, and one for me."

"Oh. I thought that the two of you . . . I mean I just assumed . . . Of course, sir." The clerk reached back for another key as Longarm glared at him. "Right away, sir. Two rooms. Fine rooms, if I do say so myself, and I should know because I'm the proprietor of this establishment. Lawrence Miller, sir, at your service."

Longarm grunted. "Pleased to meet you." He took the pen from its holder and scrawled his name and that of Emily in the register, adding *Denver* beside each of them.

Miller slid the keys across the desk. "There you go, rooms seven and eight, right at the top of the stairs. The finest accommodations in Trinidad, I assure you."

"Reckon they'll do for the night."

"You're just staying one night in our town?" The hotelkeeper was trying to be ingratiating now, but Longarm just found him annoying, like a burr under a saddle.

"That's right."

"Leaving on the southbound stage, are you? I assume that's how you got here." Miller looked at a clock on the wall. "Old Cougar's running a little late tonight."

"There was some trouble up in Pueblo." Longarm picked up the keys to the rooms and gave in to the temptation to needle Miller. "Some fellas tried to kill me before I got on board the stage. Sure hope nobody else tries to bushwhack me again tonight. Be a shame if one of the rooms in this fine establishment of yours got shot all to pieces."

He took Emily's arm and led her up the stairs, leaving Miller to gawk after them.

Emily laughed softly as they reached the landing. "That was terrible," she told Longarm.

"Yeah, I reckon. But that old son got under my skin." He tried one of the keys in the knob of room seven. It worked on the first try. "Here you go."

Emily stepped into the room and turned to look back at him for a moment. "Thank you, Marshal. You don't know what it means to me to have you looking out for me. Things have been so . . . so confused lately."

"They'll all work out," he assured her.

Emily smiled. "For the first time in quite a while, I think perhaps they will. Good night, Marshal."

"Good night, miss," Longarm said. He waited there in the hall until the door of Emily's room clicked shut.

Then he turned and went to his own room next door. He went in carefully, as he went into every room he entered, but no gunmen lurked inside. In fact, the rest of the night passed peacefully, though it was a while before Longarm was able to go to sleep.

He found himself lying in bed thinking about blond hair, blue eyes, and the soft touch of a female hand. He could still smell the scent of her perfume.

It was a damned shame he still had the stink of burned gunpowder in his nose, too.

The view from the top of Raton Pass was a mighty nice one. Mountains to the east and west, the town of Raton nestled in the foothills to the south, plains to the southeast that rolled all the way to the Texas Panhandle. The stage was in New Mexico Territory now, having crossed the border from Colorado a short time earlier. With a shout to his team, Cougar Powell sent the stagecoach rolling down the sloping road toward the bottom of the pass.

Longarm and Emily braced their feet and hung on as the coach tilted. "Ever been this way?" Longarm asked his companion with a grin.

"Not going down," Emily answered nervously. "When my father took me to Denver, we came this way, of course, but we were going up. All I remember is that it was a long, slow climb."

"It'll be faster going down," Longarm told her. "Too fast if that old vinegaroon on the box don't mind what he's doing."

Cougar handled the team of horses expertly, however, and he had a sure, experienced hand on the vehicle's brake. The coach descended at a rapid but not reckless pace.

Earlier that morning at breakfast in the hotel dining room, Longarm had found that Emily had had a peaceful night, too. After eating, he settled up the bill for both of them, ignoring Emily's offer to pay for her own room. Uncle Sam could pick up the tab, he assured her, since she was helping him with official business.

"But I'm not even supposed to be here," she had reminded him. "I ran away from your friend Henry up in Denver."

Longarm had refrained from pointing out to her that he and Henry weren't exactly what you could call friends. Friendly adversaries, maybe. But they were, admittedly, on the same side in the fight for law and order.

"That don't matter. The way it's worked out, you and me are partners now, until we find that stolen gold."

Emily had smiled. "Partners. I like the sound of that, Marshal."

"In which case, I reckon you ought to call me Custis."

"All right. And I'm Emily."

"A pretty name for a pretty gal." Longarm knew he was flirting shamelessly, but Emily didn't seem to mind. And she didn't even know what had happened between them on the previous evening during the stagecoach ride from Pueblo to Trinidad . . .

The coach swayed and rocked and finally reached the bottom of the pass. Cougar popped his whip over the backs of the team and shouted at them. The horses broke into a gallop for the last stretch run into Raton. A few minutes later, the coach rolled along the street between respectable brick and stone buildings and came to a stop in front of the station.

Longarm climbed out and helped Emily to the ground. As he unloaded their gear from the boot, he said to her, "I'll rent us some horses and pick up some supplies. Do you have any clothes better for riding than those you've got on?"

"No, but there's a general store right over there," Emily replied. "I'll go buy a few things while you're busy with the horses. I can get the clerk to start packing our supplies, too."

"Not too much in the way of provisions," Longarm cautioned. "We'll have to travel a little light, since I don't want to take a pack mule along."

"I understand. I won't get any more than we can carry in a couple of pairs of saddlebags."

"I reckon you'll need a sidesaddle?"

Emily laughed scornfully. "Hardly. How many times do I have to tell you, Custis, I'm a western girl. I can manage astride just fine."

"Well, if you say so." Longarm's tone was a mite dubious.

Emily walked over to the general store. Longarm placed their bags and his saddle on the boardwalk in front of the station. Cougar came over to him and said, "Reckon this is where we part trails again, Custis. I hope it won't be as long 'fore we see each other again as it was this time."

Longarm took the callused paw that the old-timer stuck out at him. "Me, too," he said as they shook. "So long, Cougar."

With a wave, Cougar turned to see to the changing of the coach's team, while Longarm strode down the street toward the nearest livery stable. Ten minutes of bargaining with the stable's proprietor bought the rent of two horses and a saddle for the mount that Emily would ride, as well as a pair of saddlebags for each horse and a boot for Longarm's Winchester. He chose a rangy buckskin gelding for himself and picked a chestnut for Emily that looked like a steady-nerved animal. They would be riding some high, narrow trails as they crossed the mountains, and he didn't want Emily on a horse that was likely to spook. He wasn't convinced yet that she was as good a rider as she thought she was.

When the horses were saddled and ready to ride, he led them down the street to the general store where Emily had gone. He didn't see her waiting for him. There was a boy standing on the business's porch, but that was all.

Suddenly, Longarm stopped in his tracks as he realized that was no boy. Not shaped like that it wasn't. A moment later the figure turned and waved at him.

Emily wore a flat-crowned black hat, a man's checked work shirt with the sleeves rolled up a couple of turns, and denim trousers with the legs tucked into high-topped black boots. The fabric of the trousers clung to the curves of her thighs and hips with loving snugness. The shirtfront was filled out nicely by the thrust of high, firm breasts. All in all, Emily looked about as good in man's clothes as any gal Longarm had ever seen, with the possible exception of his old pal Jessie Starbuck, who had been born to wear tight denim trousers.

Emily stepped down off the porch and said, "Ready to ride, Custis?"

In more ways than one, thought Longarm, but he just nodded. The mountains were waiting for them . . . and so was whatever was on the other side.

Chapter 7

Starting out, they rode south from Raton for several hours before curving westward toward the mountains. Longarm remembered an old trail that followed a stream through the foothills and then high into the peaks, where the creek had its origins. From there it was a short climb up a narrow path to a pass that would take them through to the other side of the Sangre de Cristos. It was a one-way trail, with room enough for only a single horse at a time. Longarm kept an eye on Emily as she rode, trying to judge if she was capable of handling where they were going.

She seemed at home in the saddle, swaying gently and easily with the rhythm of the chestnut's gait. After a while, Longarm said, "Somehow, I don't figure you dressed like that and rode astride back in Philadelphia."

"No," Emily replied with a laugh. "I certainly didn't. Back there it was a sidesaddle and only the most stylish riding habits."

"What would Miss Van Der Houton say if she could see you now?"

"The poor old dear would probably faint!"

They laughed together. Longarm enjoyed the easy camaraderie that had sprung up between them, despite the short time they had known each other. At the same time, he kept a close eye on their surroundings and checked their back trail pretty often. There was no sign of an ambush or other trouble. They seemed to have the entire New Mexico Territory to themselves, though he knew that wasn't true.

They reached the creek he was looking for and turned almost due west to follow it. The terrain grew more rugged as they began to climb through the foothills. The mountains loomed ahead, tall and majestic against the blue sky. A few puffy white clouds floated over the peaks. To the right of Longarm and Emily, the stream brawled and bubbled and chuckled along its rocky bed. He spotted an eagle circling through the sky and pointed it out to her. In a pleased voice, Emily said, "How beautiful! I had almost forgotten what it's like out here."

"This western country gets inside a fella," Longarm mused as he rode along beside her. "There's so danged much to see, and even the places that ain't particularly pretty have something about them that makes you want to stop and just look at 'em for a while. I know that when I first came out here, it didn't take me long to realize I'd found the place I was meant to be."

"Where did you come from?" she asked curiously.

"Was born and raised in West-by-God Virginia. After the war, though, I didn't feel much like going back and trying to farm. So I headed west like so many other young fellas about that time."

"You were in the Civil War?"

"Yeah, but don't ask me which side I was on. I disremember. Once it was all over, it didn't really matter anyway."

"My father was in the war," Emily said. "He rode with a man named Forrest."

Longarm nodded. "General Nathan Bedford Forrest, Confederate cavalry. One of the best officers in the war on either side, from what I hear. Maybe the best natural cavalry leader of them all, even better than Jeb Stuart or Custer."

"You must have been a Confederate," Emily said. "You sound like you admire General Forrest."

"You can admire a good fighting man whether you're on his side or not," Longarm pointed out.

"I suppose that's true. Father thought the world of General Forrest, I know that. I remember listening as a little girl while he talked about Shiloh and all the other battles he was in."

They rode on, stopping for lunch at midday while they were still fairly low in the foothills. Longarm fried bacon and made biscuits in the small frying pan he took from the warbag that was tied on behind his saddle. Emily watched with admiration. "You're quite a trail cook," she commented.

"Out here, a fella's got to learn to do lots of different things if he wants to get along and take care of himself. You ought to see me handle a needle and thread."

Emily laughed. "Maybe I'll get a chance to."

After they had eaten and the horses had rested, they resumed the journey. The sun high overhead was warm, but a cool breeze drifted down from the mountains and kept them from getting too hot. It was a perfect day, Longarm thought, and he was spending it with the perfect companion. That made him nervous. Whenever things seemed to be going good, they usually went to hell in a hay wagon with little or no warning.

Not today, though. The rest of the afternoon passed without incident, and nightfall found them making camp beside the creek, under a stand of pines.

Longarm kept the fire small, cooked supper quickly, and then extinguished the flames. Already, the air was cool now that the sun was down, and the warmth of a fire would have felt good. But he didn't want to announce their presence too blatantly. Just because he hadn't seen anyone trailing them all day didn't mean nobody was following them.

Of course, the hombres who wanted to stop them from getting where they were going might be in front of them, instead of behind. Emily's talking of Bedford Forrest and the war made Longarm think of the situation in military terms. The enemy was fighting a defensive action, trying to keep Longarm from advancing to a strategic position. That meant Longarm had to fight them on ground of their own choosing. That was going to put him at a disadvantage unless he could draw them out some way.

"You're awfully quiet tonight, Custis," Emily said. She laughed softly. "Not that I would really know, I suppose. We've only been acquainted for a little over a day, so I don't know what you're normally like, do I?"

"Oh, I ain't sure of that." Longarm leaned back on an elbow. "I ain't what you'd call a complicated sort of fella. The way folks see me is pretty much the way I am."

"I doubt that. I think you're an intelligent man, despite the rustic facade you put on."

"Rustic facade," Longarm repeated wryly. "I been accused of having a heap of things, but I don't reckon that's ever been one of them until now."

"See, that's exactly what I'm talking about. You act as if you're just an unlettered frontiersman, but I'd wager you're well-educated."

"That's where you'd be wrong. I never finished school."

"But you read, don't you? You're self-taught."

Longarm shrugged. "I been known to pay a visit to the public library. Fella's got to do something for entertainment along toward the end of the month when the last paycheck's done run out." He didn't mention the fact that one of the gals who clerked at the library was mighty

71

pretty, even before she took off her spectacles. Friendly, too, when she was of a mind to be.

"I knew it. What's the last book you read?"

"Lemme think . . . It was a book of stories and poems by that Poe gent."

"Edgar Allan Poe? His stories are quite . . . bizarre, don't you think?"

"Sometimes. He's a mite long-winded, too. But pretty entertaining, I reckon."

"And quite poignant. In 'The Raven,' when the narrator speaks of his lost Lenore, it's almost enough to bring tears to my eyes."

"Nevermore," muttered Longarm.

"What was that?"

He waved a hand. "Nothin' Just thinking about how life can be a mite odd. I mean, here I am in a trail camp in the foothills of the Sangre de Cristos, talking to the prettiest gal I've seen in a long time about Edgar Allan Poe, of all things."

Longarm couldn't see Emily all that well in the shadows, but from the tone of her voice, he thought she might be blushing as she said, "Really? You think I'm the prettiest girl you've seen in a long time?"

"Your pa got his money's worth from Miss Van Der Houton. You're quite a lady, Emily."

"Oh. Yes, I suppose so. About the money, I mean."

Her voice was suddenly much cooler, and Longarm could have kicked himself for bringing up her father and the money he had paid for her schooling, because that reminded Emily of all the bad things, including the fact that Clete Harrigan was a bank robber.

"I think I'll turn in now," Emily went on. She began to spread her bedroll on the far side of the campfire's ashes.

"I'll stand first watch," Longarm said.

She hesitated. "We have to stand watch?"

72

"I reckon it'd be a good idea. We don't want anything sneaking up on us, man or animal."

"Of course. You're right, Custis. Wake me when it's time for me to take my turn."

"I'll do that," he promised. He meant it, too. He had to find out sometime if he could rely on Emily. From everything he had seen so far, he believed that he could, but he didn't know for sure. He would give her the chance to prove herself.

Longarm propped his back against a rock, chewed on an unlit cheroot, and sat with his Winchester between his knees for the next several hours. Overhead, the pinpricks of dancing light that marked the stars wheeled on their mysterious courses through the heavens. Small animals rustled in the brush along the creek. Somewhere not far off, an owl hooted. In the distance, a wolf howled. Longarm was content.

The middle of the night came and went. Longarm still felt alert, so he allowed Emily to sleep longer. He didn't decide to wake her until he realized that he was getting drowsy. He stood up, walked quietly around the fire, and knelt beside her. With a gentle touch on her shoulder, he said her name.

She came up out of sleep with a startled jerk. Her arms went around his neck and pulled. Hunkered on his heels the way he was, he had no chance of keeping his balance. He toppled forward, landing right on top of her. She screamed and let go of his neck with one arm so that she could use that fist to hit him. Longarm grabbed her wrist to stop her, even though the blows weren't doing any damage.

"Emily!" he said sharply. "Stop that! It's just me, Custis Long."

She continued writhing underneath him for a couple more seconds, then abruptly grew still, as if his words had just penetrated her brain. She was breathing hard, her chest heaving so that her breasts were flattened under Longarm's weight. He got a hand on the ground and pushed himself up a little so that he wouldn't crush her.

"Custis?" she asked in a whisper.

"Yep. Everything's all right, Emily. You don't have to be afraid."

She still had one arm looped around his neck. The other arm joined it, and once again she pulled him down to her. She wasn't fighting him now, though. Their lips met, and it quickly became obvious that she wasn't interested in fighting at all.

Longarm wasn't sure what was going on here, but he could count on the fingers of one hand the times in his life when he had refused to kiss a pretty girl who wanted to be kissed. Emily had lifted her head from the ground when she brought her mouth to his. Now he slipped his hand under her head, cushioning it. The kiss was hard and hungry at first, but then it softened, became gentler. Her lips parted. Longarm slipped his tongue between them to explore the hot, wet sweetness of her mouth. Her tongue circled his in a tender caress.

He felt her nipples through her shirt, hard and erect against his chest. He brought his other hand up her side and covered her right breast, squeezing gently. His thumb found her nipple, stroked the pebbled bud of flesh. Emily whimpered deep in her throat.

Somehow, her legs had parted and he found himself lying between them. Her pelvis came up into his groin with a hard thrust. Instinctively, he returned the move. Both of them were still fully clothed, though, so all they could do in this position was dry-hump each other.

They had better do something about that, Longarm decided.

He found the buttons of her shirt and deftly began unfastening them. He spread the garment open and cupped her now-bare breast. At the same time, Emily sought and found the buttons on his trousers and started opening them. All the while, they continued the kiss, which was becoming more heated and urgent again.

Longarm had laid the Winchester aside, but it was still close by if he needed it. Emily was having some trouble with his trousers because of the gunbelt around his hips. He pushed himself up, feeling a momentary pang of regret as their mouths parted. He unfastened the belt and set it aside, next to the rifle. With that obstacle removed, Emily was able to finish loosening his trousers. She shoved them down over his hips, then slipped her hand underneath the bottoms of his long underwear to close her fingers around his rock-hard shaft.

Longarm's body stiffened at the heat of her grip. It had felt good the night before through his clothes, but it felt even better now with nothing between them but skin. Emily stroked up and down the thick pole and breathed, "Oh, my God, there's so much of you, Custis."

He had her pants unfastened by now. He pulled them down over her thighs, taking the long underwear with them. She raised her bottom off the bedroll to make it easier for him. He pulled the garments all the way down. She had taken off her boots before she turned in, so it was no problem for her to kick the trousers and underwear off her legs. With her shirt unbuttoned and wide open the way it was, she was more naked than not. She continued to fondle his manhood as he lowered his head to her breasts and sucked and licked each nipple in turn.

With his head pressed against her that way, he could hear her heart beating. Her pulse hammered fast and hard, a definite reflection of the excitement she was experiencing. Longarm moved down her body, licking and kissing, leaving a heated trail where his tongue explored her. Her already open legs spread even wider in invitation. Longarm cupped his hand over the mound at the juncture of her thighs. It was covered with fine, silky hair, and when

75

he dipped a finger below it, he found that the folds of flesh at the gates of her sex were already wet with dew. His finger speared into her, making her cry out as her hips lurched off the ground again.

Longarm added a second finger to the first one and used his thumb to tease the hard nubbin at the top of her opening. After several minutes of these caresses, he knelt between her thighs and brought his mouth to her femininity. He replaced his fingers with his tongue. She grabbed hold of his head, raking her fingers through his thick, dark brown hair. Her legs locked together behind his neck, the thighs pressing warmly against his ears, as if she were trying to engulf him. Her hips bounced up and down on the bedroll in time to the cries of passion that escaped from her lips. Skillfully, Longarm prodded her higher and higher on the mountain she was climbing, until she finally reached the crest and trembled violently with the culmination of the ecstasy she was feeling. When it was over at last, she sagged back on the bedroll with every muscle in her body limp and satiated.

Longarm gave her a few moments to catch her breath. Her legs were splayed wide again. He kissed the insides of her thighs as he gradually lifted himself higher. When he was in position, he brought the head of his erect organ to her drenched opening and rested it there for a second, long enough for Emily to realize that their lovemaking wasn't over yet. She opened her eyes and raised her head from the ground. Longarm's hips surged forward. The long, thick shaft of male flesh penetrated her, sliding easily into her sheath. Emily cried out in a mixture of pain and delight as he filled her. She was tight, so tight that Longarm knew she had never before experienced a man of such generous proportions. She wasn't a virgin, though. He had deflowered a few gals in his life and knew what that felt like.

He began pumping in and out of her in the timeless,

universal rhythm of man and woman coupling. Emily raised her knees higher so that he could reach even deeper inside her. She clasped her arms around his neck. Longarm kissed her, and this time she drove her tongue into his mouth. He knew she had to taste her own juices on his lips and tongue, and that seemed to drive her even wilder. Her hips bucked hard against him as he pounded into her.

The pace was so urgent for both of them that the experience couldn't last very long. Longarm felt his climax building and held it off for a few moments, but the need to reach the peak was almost overwhelming. He had to give in to it. From the way Emily was moaning and gasping and thrashing under him, he knew that she was ready for what he had to give her. So with a final thrust, he buried his shaft as deep in her core as he could and let it all wash over him. He jerked and shuddered as his seed exploded out of him in spurt after white-hot spurt. He filled her until she was overflowing around him. Emily spasmed as a second climax rippled through her.

Despite the coolness of the night, both of them were covered with a fine sheen of sweat. With the two of them still joined together, Longarm drew the blankets around them so they wouldn't catch a chill. He leaned down and kissed Emily's eyes and nose and chin before pressing his lips to hers again.

"I never dreamed . . ." she murmured. "I just never dreamed it could be like that . . ."

Longarm rolled onto his side, taking her with him. His softening organ slipped out of her, but he still held her close. He stroked her back and her flanks. She was still trembling.

She raised her head, and he saw her looking at him in the starlight. "Remember what you asked me earlier? What would Miss Van Der Houton think?" she whispered with a mischievous grin.

"She'd probably be a mite jealous," Longarm said.

A laugh burst out of Emily. "You're probably right." She rested her head against his shoulder. "I can't believe I was so . . . so bold. I swear to you, Custis, I don't normally do . . . that . . . with men I've known for less than thirty-six hours."

"I figured as much. To tell you the truth, I'm glad you ain't upset with me. I sort of felt like I took advantage of you."

"I was the one who grabbed you first, remember?"

"Yeah, but you were spooked, the way I woke you up like that."

Emily's fingers reached into his shirt and stroked the thick mat of hair on his chest. "I was having a nightmare," she said quietly. "I thought . . . I thought that man I killed last night up at Pueblo had come back to get me."

"Killing's never easy," he told her. "I've had to do a heap of it over the years since I pinned on a lawman's badge, but I never have got to where I liked it. Thank God."

"Does . . . does it give you nightmares?"

"Not so's you'd notice. A shootist name of Clay Allison, down on the Cimarron, once said he never killed anybody who didn't need killin'. I don't know if that's true or not, but I know I never shot anybody unless it was to protect my own life or the life of somebody else. Anytime I get a mite restless at night, I can think about that and know that I at least tried to do the right thing."

"And you think that's what I did?"

"Considering the fact that that old son had just put a bullet within a few inches of my ear, you're damned right I think so," he said. "If you hadn't blasted him with that scattergun, I'd have ventilated him with my Colt about a second later."

"Or he would have killed you."

"Yeah, that's possible, too. So you see, I don't think

78

you need to be having bad dreams about what happened. There's a good chance you saved my life, and I'm mighty grateful."

She moved her hand down his belly. "Is that what you were demonstrating tonight?" she asked as she cupped his shaft. "Gratitude?"

"Well, not really. Mostly, you just make me randy as all get-out."

Emily laughed and moved her hand up and down as he stiffened under her sensuous touch. "Yes, I believe I do. I must have quite an effect on you for this to be happening again already." She squeezed him as she leaned her mouth close to his ear and whispered, "I believe I'll go inspect the situation from a closer angle."

"You do that, ma'am," Longarm told her. He held the blanket up so that she could turn around and slide her head down next to his groin. The head of his shaft nudged her lips. She opened her mouth and took it in.

Longarm closed his eyes and lay back to enjoy what she was doing to him. He knew he would be tired when it came time to start down the trail again in the morning . . . but it would be a good tired.

Chapter 8

Longarm finally got a couple of hours of sleep not long before dawn. When he woke, the sun was up and birds were singing in the trees. The smell of bacon frying and coffee boiling filled the air. Wrapped in warm blankets, Longarm sighed. Those sensations were just about the most pleasant that a fella could experience. He was of a good mind to just lie there and enjoy them for a few minutes, the sort of luxuriating that he rarely got to do.

That sense of relaxation might have been why it was doubly jarring when a frightened scream suddenly rang out, shattering the peaceful morning.

He rolled over, throwing the blankets aside as he lunged toward the coiled gunbelt lying only a couple of feet away on the carpet of pine needles under the trees. He had pulled his trousers back on before going to sleep, so at least he wasn't naked. The morning air was cold on his bare chest as he snagged the butt of the Colt and came to his feet.

A rifle barked somewhere close by, followed a second later by a flurry of shots farther away. Emily cried out again. Longarm looked for her but couldn't find her. Then another close shot sounded, and the puff of smoke that accompanied it drew his eye to a fallen tree close to the edge of the creek. He saw a flash of sunlight off blond hair as she ducked down again.

Something whipped past Longarm's head as more shots rang out. The peace of the morning had long since been shattered. He regretted that. He regretted even more the fact that some sons of bitches were trying to kill him. A slug kicked up dirt and pine needles only inches from his feet as he broke into a run toward the fallen tree where Emily had taken cover.

She rose up with his Winchester and fired again over the deadfall. "Hurry, Custis!" she called to him.

He didn't need any extra encouragement. The bullets buzzing around him like angry hornets provided plenty. He left his feet in a leap as he reached the tree, vaulting over it. He sprawled on the other side, rolling onto his belly and crawling closer to the thick trunk. Splinters rained down on him as slugs chewed into the pine. Emily cried out in fear as she pressed herself as close to the ground as possible. Longarm followed suit. The tree was the best cover around, but he wouldn't have minded if the trunk had been a little thicker.

"Are you all right?" he asked her a moment later when he had caught his breath.

"I'm not hit. I spotted them just before they opened fire and jumped behind this tree as fast as I could. I'm sorry there was no time to warn you, Custis."

Longarm shook his head. "Don't worry about that. Did you see how many of the bastards there are?"

"No, not for sure. I saw two men, I think, but it sounds like there are at least three rifles over there."

Longarm listened to the continuing fusillade and after a second nodded in agreement. "I make it three, all right," he said. "On that knoll over yonder, about eighty yards away?"

"That's right. I saw a flash of light . . . I don't know where it came from—"

"Sunlight on a rifle barrel or belt buckle, more'n likely," he put in.

"Yes, probably. When I looked up because of the flash, I saw two men with rifles. They ducked behind trees and raised their guns. That . . . that's when I screamed. I knew they were going to attack us. So I shot at them first."

Longarm frowned. Chances were, the hombres over there on the knoll were more of the same breed of hired killer as the men in Denver and the ones at Pueblo. But there was a slim chance they *hadn't* been sneaking up on the camp to bushwhack him and Emily. If that were the case, then he couldn't blame them for shooting back when she opened fire.

But he couldn't very well ask the gents if they were cold-blooded killers or just innocent drifters. He didn't even dare to lift his head the way they were throwing lead. From the sound of it, they planned to use bullets to whittle that fallen tree away to nothing. They had made a good start on it already.

Emily had fired the Winchester three times. That left a dozen rounds in it. He had the Colt with five bullets in its cylinder, but the range was too great for a handgun to be of much use. All the other ammunition was a good twenty feet away, in the saddlebags over by the ashes of the previous evening's small fire. Longarm figured if he made a try for the saddlebags, he wouldn't get halfway there before the riflemen on the knoll ventilated him.

"I . . . I was going down to the creek to get water for coffee," Emily said. "I just happened to look back . . . well, actually, I was watching you sleep . . . and then I saw those men . . . Maybe I shouldn't have shot at them."

"If you hadn't started the ball, I reckon they would have in another minute or two," he told her. "You did fine, Emily."

"But now we're trapped here!"

"Pretty much," Longarm said. It wouldn't do any good to deny that they were pinned down. Things didn't look very good.

So it came as no surprise to him a second later when they got even worse.

The sound of pounding hoofbeats came from somewhere downstream. Longarm jerked his head around to peer in that direction. The creek made a bend about a hundred yards away. Around that bend came two men on horseback, galloping in the stream itself as they charged toward Longarm and Emily. They had six-guns in their hands and started blazing away as soon as they saw their quarry huddled against the fallen pine.

Longarm grated out a curse and snatched the Winchester out of Emily's hands. He rolled over onto his belly and snugged the butt of the rifle against his bare shoulder. At this range, the revolvers used by the two men riding toward them were pretty inaccurate and were made more so by the fact that the men were firing from horseback. However, as far as Longarm was concerned, this flanking attack answered the question of whether or not the men on the knoll had had bushwhacking in mind when they came skulking around the camp not long after dawn. So he didn't hesitate at all to line the Winchester's sights on the barrel chest of one of the riders and blow the son of a bitch out of the saddle.

As the 44-40 slug bored through the man's body and knocked him backward, Longarm worked the rifle's lever and shifted the sights. The second man was covering ground in a hurry. His mount's hooves splashed loudly in the creek and threw a spray of water high in the air around him. The way the droplets sparkled so brilliantly in the early morning sunlight, Longarm thought it might have made a pretty scene if the varmint hadn't been trying to kill him.

The man emptied his six-gun at Longarm and Emily, but the bullets passed harmlessly several feet over their heads. Longarm fired the rifle again and saw the rider sway in the saddle. He managed to stay on the horse, though, and even drew a second gun. He was only about twenty yards from them now and still closing fast. Longarm jacked another round into the Winchester's chamber and drew a bead. A bullet plowed up ground less than five feet in front of him. He ignored the shower of dirt in his face as best he could, blinked his eyes to clear away some of the grit, and pressed the trigger as the sights settled on the rider's chest. The rifle blasted, kicking hard against his shoulder.

The shot was a little high. It caught the man in the throat. Blood sprayed in the air as hot lead ripped through veins and arteries. He flung his arms out to the sides and toppled off the horse to the right. That foot caught in the stirrup. The horse kept running at first, dragging the body through the shallow water, but then the weight made the animal slow and stop. The creek flowed around the corpse, turning pink as blood washed out into it.

"Custis!" Emily cried.

He twisted around on the ground and saw that she had picked up the Colt he'd set aside when he took the Winchester from her. She thrust the revolver over the top of the log, holding it with both hands, and started to blaze away with it. He pushed himself up and risked a glance. The three men on the knoll had taken advantage of the distraction provided by the men on horseback to rush the deadfall. They were closing in now, firing their rifles from the hip as they came. Emily's shots made them split up, two veering to the left while the third man went to the right.

Longarm snapped the rifle to his shoulder and fired at the two on the left. A small branch flew from one of the pines, clipped off by the bullet. The two gunmen reached the safety of the trees. So did their companion to the right. Emily still pulled the trigger on the Colt, even though she was out of bullets. The hammer clicked harmlessly each time it fell. Longarm put a hand on her shoulder and shoved her down as the bushwhackers opened up again, their rifles spewing flaming death toward the fallen tree.

Nine shots left in the Winchester, Longarm calculated automatically. And the Colt was empty now. The would-be killers were closer and still had plenty of cover. Despite the fact that Longarm had downed the two who had galloped up the creek at them, he figured that the situation in which he and Emily found themselves was actually worse than it had been a few minutes earlier.

"Custis, what are we going to do?" Emily asked in a half-moan that he had trouble hearing over the rolling thunder of the rifle fire that still ate away at the fallen tree.

Longarm didn't have an answer for her. He would continue to put up a fight, but soon he would be out of ammunition. When that happened, the fight was over. The bushwhackers could close in and finish them off at their leisure.

His brain cast about desperately for an idea, and suddenly, the glimmering of one was there. The firing dwindled for a few seconds, probably because a couple of the riflemen were reloading, and he risked a swift look over the top of the log. As his head came up, all three of the bushwhackers opened up again and he had to duck frantically. He had seen enough, though, to pinpoint their locations. All three of the men were hidden in the shadows underneath the pines, just beyond the campsite.

Longarm jammed a hand into one of the pockets of his denim trousers. Their fate depended on what he found there. He felt a surge of hope as his fingers closed around a small bundle of lucifers.

Normally he kept his matches in his jacket pocket, but

often he stashed a few in his trousers as well, so that he could light a cheroot even if he wasn't wearing the jacket. Now he pulled out the lucifers and placed them on the ground in front of him. It had been a while since the pine tree had fallen, and the part that lay against the ground was rotting. He dug his hand into the soft wood and raked some of it into a pile. Then he crawled a few feet along the trunk until he could reach a protruding branch a couple of feet long and about as thick as his wrist. He grasped firmly and wrenched it off. The branch made a cracking sound as it came free.

Emily watched him, wide-eyed with fear and confusion, as he scooted back toward her. She had no idea what he was doing. He wasn't sure it would work, either, but it was their only chance, so he had to try. He picked up the sulfur matches and used his thumbnail to snap one of them into life. He held the flame to the little pile of rotten wood he had scraped up.

The wood caught fire instantly. Longarm raked up more of the rotten stuff around the flames, feeding the blaze until it burned strongly. Pungent smoke rose from it. The shooting died away again for a moment, and Longarm figured the riflemen were looking at the smoke and wondering what the hell he was doing back there behind the fallen tree. Sending up smoke signals for help, maybe . . . ?

He thrust one end of the broken branch into the fire. The bark was very dry and blazed up right away. Longarm turned the branch slowly, spreading the fire until the interior of the branch was burning, too. It wasn't much of a torch, but it would have to do. He extended his arm, holding the burning branch out at the end of it.

Then he threw it over the top of the log, sending it sailing across the campsite toward the trees where the riflemen were hidden.

The shooting stopped again and one of the men yelled,

"Shit!" Longarm risked a glance. The makeshift torch had fallen at the edge of the trees. The carpet of dried pine needles extended that far, and even though the flames from the branch threatened to sputter out, some of the needles were already burning. The flames began to spread.

"Put out that fire!" one of the men yelled. The man on the right darted from cover, evidently intending to stomp out the flames.

Longarm had been waiting for that. He fired in the blink of an eye and was rewarded by the sight of the man tumbling off his feet. Then he had to duck again because the other two started blazing away at the fallen tree. They had forgotten about him for a second, and one of them had paid the price for that.

But there were still two of them. Longarm was still outgunned. Now, though, he had an ally . . . a burning, smoking ally that continued to spread under the trees.

No frontiersman liked to see a wildfire, let alone be responsible for starting one. But the only chance Longarm and Emily had to survive was to force the riflemen out of their cover. The only way to do that was to burn it around them. The flames spread quickly, fiery tendrils shooting off from the main blaze, snaking ever deeper into the woods. Gray smoke billowed up and filled the air, coiling around the tree trunks. In a matter of minutes, the hidden riflemen would be forced to retreat. Longarm hoped that would give him and Emily a chance to grab their horses and get out of there.

That was assuming, of course, that the horses would still be there. The animals had been spooked already by all the shooting. Now with the smell of fire and death in the air, they were more crazed than ever. They danced around nervously at the end of the ropes that bound them to some saplings on the creek bank.

Longarm expected the two remaining killers to pull back, but he knew they might decide to attack instead. So

87

it didn't come as a complete surprise to him when the men burst out of the smoke, screaming curses and firing their rifles as fast as they could work the levers and pull the triggers. "Stay down!" Longarm yelled at Emily as he rose on his knees to meet the charge. The Winchester bucked against his shoulder as he fired over the top of the log.

One of the attackers went down. The next heartbeat, something burned along the upper part of the big lawman's left arm. The impact was enough to knock Longarm halfway around, and it deadened that arm, making it useless. He had just jacked the Winchester's lever when he was hit, so there was still a round in the chamber. He caught himself before he fell and lifted the rifle again, one-handed this time. It took all his strength to aim the Winchester and pull the trigger just as the remaining bushwhacker fired again.

The killer's slug whined past Longarm's ear, singing a song that had gotten damned tiresome lately. The lawman's bullet found its target, thudding into the bushwhacker's chest and driving him backward. The man fell heavily, landing with his head in the edge of the flames that ate at the pine needles. The fact that he didn't move even when his hair caught on fire told Longarm that he was dead.

Longarm stood up. He had lost track of how many shots he had fired, but he thought there were still a couple of rounds in the Winchester. His left arm, numb at first, was starting to hurt like blazes now as blood trickled a warm trail down it, but he was able to force the muscles to function again. He managed to work the rifle's lever and held the weapon ready to fire as he hurried forward. One of the two men he'd shot earlier hadn't emerged from the fire, and the sickly-sweet stench mixed with the more aromatic smoke was mute testimony about that one's fate. The second man lay clear of the flames for the moment.

Longarm approached him and saw the glassy-eyed stare. The third man's hair was still burning. All three were dead, no doubt about that.

So, despite five to one odds, Longarm had emerged triumphant from this fight. Luck had been on his side. But he would need even more good fortune in the next few minutes.

He turned to look at Emily, who was staring at him over the top of the log. "Grab our gear!" he told her. "Get it all down by the creek, and be ready to jump in if the flames come this way!"

For a second, she didn't respond, but when he said her name, she jerked a nod and hurried to do as he had told her. While she climbed over the log and then scurried around the camp gathering up their supplies and saddles, Longarm took the Winchester in his left hand and used his right to grasp one of the booted feet belonging to the man who lay with his head in the fire. He hauled the man away from the flames, trying not to look at the charred skull as he did so. He picked up the guns belonging to both of the dead men and took them down to the creek bank. Then he returned to the corpses and swiftly went through their pockets.

The gold double eagles he found told him the story he had expected to hear. These men had been trying to collect the bounty on his head, too. Someone was willing to pay, and pay dearly, to keep him from reaching Sweetwater Canyon.

Longarm coughed as smoke blew in his face. He looked up and saw that the wind had shifted. The fire was coming toward the creek now. The grass along the bank was thick and green and wouldn't burn well, which would slow down the flames. The creek itself would also act as a firebreak. Sparks could still jump across and start a new fire on the other side of the stream, though. He straightened and called to Emily, "Get the horses! Be careful and don't let them bolt!"

He went over to the pile of gear and picked up as much of it as he could, including his hat and shirt and saddlebags. He waded across the creek and dumped the stuff on the far bank, then went back for more. While he was doing that, Emily approached the horses, spoke to them quietly and gently for a moment to calm them down, then untied them and led them across the creek.

"Take them back about a hundred yards and tie them up," Longarm told her. "Then help me get the rest of this gear."

"All right, Custis." She went to work without hesitation and without complaining.

Ten minutes later, the horses were out of danger and Longarm and Emily had transferred all their gear to the other side of the creek, along with the guns and money he had taken from the dead bushwhackers. The wind continued to blow the flames toward the creek. The fire was about a hundred yards wide now.

Emily caught hold of Longarm's left hand. "You're hurt."

"Just grazed," he told her. He looked down at the injury, saw that the bullet had torn off some skin and plowed a shallow furrow in the flesh of his upper arm. The bleeding had almost stopped. "Daub a little whiskey on it, tie a rag around it, and it'll be fine."

"I can do that."

"Help me get my boots on first," he suggested. "If any sparks float across here, we'll need to get 'em stomped out mighty quick-like, before they catch hold good."

For the next half-hour, that's what they did, ranging up and down the stream, extinguishing the small fires started by sparks from the big blaze. That change in the wind had been mighty lucky, thought Longarm. Without it, the fire might have gone right on up the mountains and wound up burning a hell of a lot of forest and brush. An inferno like that could go on for days. Now, though, it looked like the fire would soon burn itself out along the creek.

Longarm didn't relax until he couldn't see any more flames in the burned area on the other side of the creek. It was a stretch of smoldering ashes now. When he was reasonably sure the danger was over, he allowed Emily to clean the wound on his arm and bandage it with strips of cloth she tore off a petticoat she took from her bag.

"That's a perfectly good petticoat you ruined," he told her as she finished tying the makeshift bandages.

"Don't worry about that. Where am I going to wear a petticoat out here?"

"I don't know," Longarm drawled. "I reckon you'd be pretty much a sight to behold in a petticoat and nothing else."

Emily laughed and blushed at the same time. "You must think I'm the most brazen hussy this side of the Mississippi."

"Nope. I think you're a smart, pretty gal with plenty of sand. Best kind in the world." He grinned at her, and she returned the smile as she moved closer, snuggling against him for a moment.

"I'd still like to fix breakfast for you," she whispered, "but . . . not here."

Longarm agreed. There were too many dead men around here, and now three of them were burned to a crisp instead of just one. "We'll go on upstream a ways," he told her. "With any luck, we'll get over the pass today."

He knew they couldn't depend on luck, though. Already, they had used up more than their fair share. Considering how many hombres had tried to kill him in the past three days, by all rights he ought to be dead by now. Instead, he was still alive, and nine of the gun-toting skunks had gone to their reward.

One thing you could say about it, thought Longarm, he didn't know how many enemies were arrayed against him, but he was sure enough whittling down the odds.

Chapter 9

The view from the heights was spectacular. Heavily forested mountain slopes swept down to rugged foothills, and the land continued to fall away from those hills until it leveled out into a broad green plain that extended for several score miles before rising again into another range of mountains.

Longarm and Emily paused on a jutting shoulder of ground to peer down at the western foothills of the Sangre de Cristos and the prosperous ranch land of San Luis Valley beyond. It was late the next afternoon. There had been no more trouble. The trip on up to the pass and through it had been uneventful. Longarm was thankful for that. His wounded arm was stiff and sore, but he was convinced it was going to heal just fine. Emily had taken good care of him.

Now she rose in the stirrups and searched the panorama in front of them for any sign of their destination. "I don't see anything," she said. "Nothing but miles and miles of pretty country, that is."

Longarm pointed. His keen eyes had already picked out several tendrils of smoke climbing into the sky. "Look right over there," he told her. "I reckon that must be

Sweetwater City." The settlement's location was several miles northwest from where they sat their horses. Pretty good for steering a path across the mountains by dead reckoning, he thought.

"Where's the creek and the canyon?"

Longarm lifted the reins and clucked to his mount. "Let's go see if we can find out."

They rode north through the foothills, Longarm picking the easiest route for them. Emily had done fine on the high, narrow trail to the pass. She had turned a little pale when the path skirted drop-offs of two thousand feet, but nobody could fault her for that. She'd kept her horse under control and followed steadfastly along behind Longarm. He figured that she deserved some easier going now.

They had made love again the night before, camped high in the mountains just west of the pass, bundled in blankets against the chill of the altitude. Longarm sensed a little desperation in the way Emily had clung to him as they coupled. She had been through a lot in the past few days, even for a bank robber's daughter. During that time, she had seen more violence first-hand than she had witnessed in the entire rest of her life. But she had come through it strong and resolute, and Longarm was proud of her.

As they huddled in their blankets afterward, their talk drifted to Emily's father. "I believe he must have had a real change of heart," she had said. "Even though he may never know about it, I . . . I hope he hangs on until we've recovered that gold. I think that would please him. He never really meant to be an outlaw, you know."

"What started him on the owlhoot trail?" Longarm had asked.

"The war, of course. I suppose he saw too much killing, too much blood. That does something to a man, I expect."

"He saw plenty of fighting if he was at Shiloh," Longarm commented.

Emily nodded as she rested her head on his shoulder. "Yes. He was part of one of the charges against something he called the Hornet's Nest. I've read a little about it. It must have been awful, all those boys charging right into the face of the enemy guns and being cut down like . . . like so much wheat."

Longarm had his own memories of such things. "I reckon it was bad, all right," he said solemnly.

"I remember my father saying that the Hornet's Nest was the defining moment of his life. He was capable of insights like that from time to time. He said he was never the same after that day. And then, after the war, when things were so bad for the Southerners during Reconstruction . . . I suppose he just didn't see any point in trying to be a law-abiding man anymore. He thought the world had taken away so much from him that he didn't see anything wrong with trying to take some of it back."

Longarm thought she was making excuses for Harrigan, but that was understandable. She was his daughter, after all, and loved him whether he deserved it or not. But having some bad experiences during and after the war wasn't a good enough reason for a fella to go around robbing banks and holding up trains. If it was, there wouldn't be an unrobbed bank in the whole blasted country.

Maybe she was right, though, about Harrigan having a change of heart. For Emily's sake, Longarm hoped that was the case.

After riding a short distance, they came to a creek that meandered along through the foothills, flowing fast as it made its way toward the basin. Longarm reined in and turned to look up toward the mountains. He wasn't sure, but he thought he saw a dark canyon mouth about a mile upstream. He swung down from the saddle as Emily asked, "Do you think this is it?"

Longarm hunkered on his heels next to the water and

scooped up a handful. He brought it to his mouth and drank. The water was cold, plenty cold enough to come from deep mountain springs that were augmented by snowmelt. And it had another quality to it, as well.

"Sweet," he said. "If this is Sweetwater Creek, the name fits."

Emily was about to get down from her horse and sample the water for herself when Longarm heard the swift drumming of approaching hoofbeats. He straightened quickly from his crouch and motioned for Emily to stay in the saddle, just in case they had to ride out of here in a hurry.

A group of riders emerged from a stand of trees on the far side of the creek. They came toward the stream, not galloping but not wasting any time about it, either. Longarm counted them as he eased back alongside his horse, where he could reach the Winchester in a hurry if he needed to. There were eight men in the group, all dressed in range clothes. All eight were armed, too, with pistols and rifles, but that wasn't unusual out here on the frontier. Most men carried at least one gun. All that firepower didn't mean the horsebackers were looking for trouble.

Didn't mean they weren't, either, Longarm reminded himself.

The big man who was slightly in the lead raised a hand to call a halt as the riders reached the creek. As the men reined in, the leader rested his hands on his saddlehorn and leaned forward, his keen stare studying Longarm and Emily. After a moment, he said, "I don't know who you two are, but you'd better have a damned good reason for bein' on my range."

"We didn't know it was your range," Longarm said coolly.

"Well, it damned sure is, no matter what that bastard McKendrie says!"

Longarm shook his head. "Don't reckon I know anybody named McKendrie. Just like I don't know you, mister."

The spokesman for the group of cowboys puffed up, his face turning red as he grew even angrier. He was a stocky man in late middle age, with white hair poking out from under his black Stetson and a white mustache drooping on either side of his mouth. Silvery bristles dotted his belligerent jaw.

"I'm Axel Schermerhorn, damn it! Owner of the Diamond S! Don't tell me you ain't heard of me!"

Longarm shook his head and drawled, "Afraid not, old son." The rancher was so florid-faced and swollen up by now, Longarm wondered if he was going to explode.

One of the other men edged his horse forward and held out a hand toward Schermerhorn. "Take it easy, boss," he said. "These folks don't appear to be lookin' for trouble."

"Trouble!" Schermerhorn said. "I'll give 'em trouble! Them and any other polecats Ben McKendrie sends over here to rustle my beeves!"

"They don't look like any rustlers I ever seen," the other man said. Evidently, he had experience at trying to calm down the man whose brand he rode for.

Longarm said, "We're just passing through on our way to Sweetwater City. We're going the right direction, ain't we?"

Schermerhorn's segundo nodded. "That's right, mister. Just follow this creek about five miles and you'll be there."

"Much obliged." Longarm gestured toward the stream. "I reckon this must be Sweetwater Creek, then."

"Sure enough."

Schermerhorn had kept quiet for as long as he could stand it. "Get off my land," he grated. "Get off now, or by God I'll string you up, you Injun-lookin' son of a bitch, and I'll see that your woman's locked up!"

Longarm had taken just about enough of the rancher's

abuse. Eight-to-one odds or not, anger flared inside him. Before he could say anything, though, the segundo reined his horse forward, getting between Longarm and Schermerhorn.

"Mount up and move on toward town," he said in a low, urgent voice. "I'll see that the boss and the rest of the boys don't bother you."

With an effort, Longarm reined in his temper. "That boss of yours has been in the loco weed," he said quietly as he gathered up the reins and reached for his saddlehorn.

"He's got plenty of reasons to be a mite touchy." The segundo jerked his head in the direction of the settlement. "Get movin'."

Longarm didn't like being ordered around, but at least this hombre seemed to be trying to head off trouble, rather than provoke it. He and Emily had come all this way, survived all the risks and danger, to try to find the gold her father had stashed, not to get in arguments with half-crazy cattlemen. For now, they would move on as they had been told. The problem was that they would have to cross this range again to get back to Sweetwater Canyon.

That could wait, though. Longarm stepped up into the saddle and turned his horse. With Emily beside him, he rode along the bank of the creek toward the valley. A glance behind him as they rode off told him that Axel Schermerhorn looked as furious as ever. Longarm could practically see steam coming out of the man's ears.

When they had gone a short distance, Emily said, "I thought that poor man's head was going to explode. I never saw anybody get so angry over nothing."

Longarm was able to chuckle about it now that they had put a little distance between themselves and the group of Diamond S riders. "A fella who gets that mad is liable to fret himself to death if he's not careful."

"I wonder why he was so upset."

"Sounded to me like there's some sort of range war

97

brewing between Schermerhorn and that fella McKendrie, whoever he is. Reckon we've ridden into something of a hornet's nest our ownselves. But it don't have anything to do with why we're here, so we'll just try to avoid Schermerhorn and McKendrie both."

They rode on, and as the sun dipped behind the mountains to the west and the daylight faded into dusky shadows, yellow glimmers became visible ahead of them. Those would be lighted windows in Sweetwater City, Longarm knew.

The creek led directly to the settlement. When they got there, they saw that the stream divided Sweetwater City roughly in northern and southern halves. It was spanned by a railed wooden bridge. To the north were a couple of churches and a main street bordered by respectable businesses and residences. South of the creek, the street was lined by saloons, gambling dens, and cribs. Most of the lights came from that side of town, though many of the houses on the north side showed lighted windows, too. Tinny player piano music floated out of the saloons.

Longarm and Emily were on the south side of the creek. Longarm figured they would have to go over to the north side to find a decent hotel. As they approached the bridge, he spotted a man leaning on the railing, watching them. He straightened from his casual pose and strolled down to the southern end of the bridge to meet them. Longarm and Emily reined in.

"Howdy, folks," the man said as he raised the index finger of his left hand to the brim of his hat and gave Emily a polite nod. "Ma'am." He was in his thirties, Longarm judged, and had a tin star pinned to his vest. His right hand stayed close to the butt of the gun holstered on his hip, a sure sign of a cautious man.

"Evenin'," Longarm replied. "I reckon you'd be the law hereabouts?"

"Jace Drummond," the man said, "marshal of Sweet-water City. Welcome to our community."

Longarm supplied his name without identifying himself as a deputy U.S. marshal. Then he said, "This is Miss Emily Harrigan. We're looking for a decent place we can get a couple of rooms."

"Well, there's no hotel here in town," Jace Drummond said. He rubbed his jaw in thought. "But Miz Hingerson up the street rents out rooms. Reckon she could put you up. Plan on staying long?"

Longarm shrugged. "Don't know yet. That'll all depend."

"Are you here on business or pleasure?"

"Business," Longarm said, though he didn't offer to explain what that business was.

"Good luck to you, then." Drummond pointed north. "Just go along the street a couple of blocks. Miz Hingerson's place is on the left. Tell her I sent you."

"We'll do that," Longarm promised. He hitched his horse into motion. Emily followed suit. Marshal Drummond touched his hat brim again as they rode past.

When they were out of earshot, Emily asked, "Why didn't you tell him that you're a lawman, too, Custis?"

"I like to have a look around a place before I go announcing who I am," Longarm explained. "Some folks tense up a mite when they know a federal star packer's around, especially if they've got anything to hide."

"But Marshal Drummond wouldn't have any reason to be bothered by that."

"Not that we know of. I'm in the habit of maybe being too careful, though. Goes with the job."

"If you say so. I'm just looking forward to sleeping in a real bed again." She paused, then added, "Not that the past few nights haven't been wonderful."

Longarm laughed. "I know what you mean."

Mrs. Hingerson's house was two stories, constructed of

99

heavy, whitewashed timbers. A picket fence ran in front of the small yard, and a sign on it read simply ROOMS. Longarm and Emily dismounted in front of the house, tied their horses to the gate, and went up to the porch where Longarm knocked on the door.

Mrs. Hingerson proved to be an attractive woman in her forties with graying brown hair. She invited Longarm and Emily in, listened as Longarm explained that they wanted to rent a couple of rooms for an indefinite amount of time, and then nodded smiling agreement when he added that Marshal Drummond had recommended her place. "I have to tell you, though, that I don't allow any sort of impropriety under my roof," she said. "If that's a problem, you'll just have to go elsewhere."

"Not a problem at all, ma'am," Longarm said without hesitation, even though he didn't much like the idea that he and Emily wouldn't be able to romp anymore while they were staying here. Not without sneaking around, anyway, and such behavior went against the grain for him. They would just have to control themselves. That was probably a good idea anyway. He needed to concentrate on the job at hand, not on playing slap-and-tickle with Emily.

He decided to indulge his curiosity a little by continuing, "On our way through the foothills, we ran into a fella called Schermerhorn and some of his riders. He seemed a mite unfriendly."

Mrs. Hingerson's eyes widened in surprise. "You met Axel Schermerhorn, and there wasn't trouble?"

"Well, not unless you count him threatening to hang me," Longarm said with a grin.

Mrs. Hingerson shook her head. "That man! He's like a wild animal. How did you get away from him?"

"Gent who was with him stepped in and sort of calmed things down long enough for us to ride on. I got the feeling he was Schermerhorn's ramrod."

100

"A sandy-haired man in his forties?"

"That sounds like the fella."

She nodded. "Dan Wilson. He's the foreman of the Diamond S, just as you thought. He's been with that crazy Dutchman for a long time. I suppose he knows how to handle him better than anyone else around here."

"What was wrong with him?" Emily asked. "He acted like he was almost insane."

Mrs. Hingerson motioned them into the parlor. "You might as well sit down," she told them. "It's a long story."

Longarm was tired and getting hungry, but before his job here was over, knowing what was going on in the area might prove to be important. He was willing to listen while the landlady explained the reasons behind Axel Schermerhorn's rage.

"Axel Schermerhorn was one of the first settlers in the San Luis Valley," Mrs. Hingerson said when they were all seated. Longarm and Emily took a sofa with a brocaded cover while the older woman sat in a wing chair near the fireplace. "He's been here for over thirty years. Naturally, he regards the whole valley and the foothills on both sides of it as his own private domain, even though legally he owns less than a fourth of the range he uses. He didn't mind much when several families came in and started small farms. I know there have been problems elsewhere between ranchers and farmers, but not here. Mr. Schermerhorn said there was room for some small outfits. When Ben McKendrie showed up, though, that was different. McKendrie started another ranch, and Mr. Schermerhorn didn't like the competition."

"McKendrie claimed some range that Schermerhorn thought was his?" Longarm guessed.

"Yes, that's exactly right. Mr. McKendrie filed on the grazing land in the foothills on the south side of Sweetwater Creek, all the way up to Sweetwater Canyon."

Longarm and Emily glanced at each other. "That's

where we were when Schermerhorn accused us of riding on his range," Longarm told Mrs. Hingerson.

"Well, if Ben McKendrie had come along first, he probably would have been upset with you for the same reason. He's almost as prickly as Mr. Schermerhorn. Everyone around here has known for quite some time that the friction between them might turn into open warfare."

"How long has McKendrie been in the area?"

"About five years now, I suppose. Yes, almost exactly five years, now that I think about it."

"And there hasn't been any gunplay between them?"

"Not what you'd call a real range war," Mrs. Hingerson said. "There have been some skirmishes between Diamond S cowboys and BMK riders, but that's all. No one has been killed. I'm afraid that good fortune is going to run out soon, though. One of these nights, Axel Schermerhorn is going to lead a raid on the McKendrie place and try to wipe out everyone there."

"Can't the law do anything about this?" Emily said, sounding astonished.

"The sheriff has tried, but it's a long way to the county seat. Not only that, but there are different jurisdictions involved. It's not that far to the Colorado border from here, you know. Part of the valley is over the line."

"What about Marshal Drummond?"

"He's just the town marshal," Mrs. Hingerson said. "He can't really interfere between Schermerhorn and McKendrie as long as they and their men don't cause trouble here in Sweetwater City."

Longarm nodded slowly. He had run into situations like this before. He had even been called on to settle some of them whenever federal interests were involved. More than once, he'd had to duck lead being thrown in a range war. This time, though, the job that had brought him here had nothing to do with the clash between two rival ranchers.

"We'll try to steer clear of both those old boys while

we're here," he said. "We're not looking for trouble."

"What does bring you to Sweetwater City, if you don't mind my asking, Mr. Long?"

"We're horse buyers," Longarm said, improvising an explanation. "Looking to stock a ranch up in Colorado."

Mrs. Hingerson shook her head doubtfully. "I don't know of anyone around here who's raising horses for sale."

"Well, we'll take a look around. Never know what you might turn up. But that's why we ain't sure how long we'll be staying. If we don't find what we're looking for, we'll just move on."

"Good luck." Mrs. Hingerson got to her feet. "Now, if you'd like I'll show you your rooms. Then I have to get supper on the table. My other boarders will be down soon. Meals are extra, by the way."

"That's fine, ma'am," Longarm told her. "We were wondering where we'd get something to eat, weren't we, Miss Harrigan?"

"Indeed we were, Mr. Long," Emily replied. She and Longarm followed the landlady out of the parlor and up the stairs to the second floor.

A hot meal, a good night's sleep, and come morning they would be ready to start their search for Clete Harrigan's hidden loot.

Chapter 10

The food was good, the beds in their rooms were comfortable, and when Longarm and Emily came downstairs the next morning for breakfast, both of them felt rested and refreshed. Mrs. Hingerson set a good table for breakfast, too, with platters full of bacon and scrambled eggs and stacks of flapjacks, along with molasses to pour over them. The coffee was hot and strong, and the faint taste of peppermint in the Arbuckle's told Longarm that at one time the landlady must have done the cooking for some cowboys. Every bag of Arbuckle's had a piece of peppermint placed in it for a touch of sweetness, and coffee brewed that way was a staple on chuck wagons and in ranch kitchens.

Longarm reined in his appetite to keep from eating too much. He had quite a bit of riding to do. When breakfast was over and he and Emily drifted into the parlor, he quietly offered a suggestion that he knew might meet with resistance.

"Why don't you stay here today while I take a *pasear* up to that canyon and have a look around?"

Emily frowned. "I thought the idea of me coming with you was so that I could help you look for . . . well, you

104

know what." She glanced around as if afraid that someone would overhear the conversation, but they were alone in the parlor. Mrs. Hingerson's other boarders, consisting of a couple of store clerks and a telegrapher, had left for their jobs immediately following breakfast.

"That was before we knew there was a range war about to bust out," Longarm said. "I ain't sure how safe it is up there in the foothills."

"We knew there was danger involved all along," Emily argued. "Remember what happened in Pueblo and on the other side of the mountains?"

Longarm remembered those violent incidents all too well. He said, "I know. But I reckon this trouble between Schermerhorn and McKendrie, on top of whoever was trying to stop us before, is just too much. You'll be safe here in town, and I can concentrate on doing my job."

Emily's lips tightened angrily. "So I keep you from concentrating, do I? It seems to me that if you hadn't had me along, you might not have ever gotten here, Custis."

Longarm grimaced. The hell of it was, she was right about that. She had saved his bacon at the stage station in Pueblo, and her alertness had kept those bushwhackers from sneaking up on them. She had proven that she was a smart, capable young woman.

She had also proven that if he left her behind, she was perfectly capable of following on her own. He came back to the argument that it was better to have her around so that he could keep an eye on her, rather than letting her wander around on her lonesome.

"All right," he said. "You can come along. I'll go get the horses ready to ride."

"I'll gather up our gear," Emily said, smiling at him. Her expression had a hint of smug triumph in it, but Longarm chose to ignore that.

The night before, he had put their horses in a small stable behind Mrs. Hingerson's house. Now he went out to the stable, saddled the animals, and led them around to the front of the house. When he got there, he found Marshal Jace Drummond just going through the front gate.

"Mornin', Mr. Long," the local lawman greeted Longarm. "About to head out on that business of yours?" Drummond was curious and not making much of an effort to conceal it.

"That's right," Longarm said. At that moment, Emily came out the front door of the house, saddlebags slung over her shoulder, Longarm's Winchester in her hand. She made a mighty appealing picture in those tight denims and man's shirt, thought Longarm.

Evidently, Marshal Drummond thought the same thing. Longarm saw the interest spark in the man's eyes, took note of the way Drummond's gaze lingered on the curve of Emily's hips and the thrust of her breasts. The marshal smiled and took his hat off, rather than just ticking a finger against the brim as he had done the day before.

"Good morning, Miss Harrigan," he said, greeting her more formally than he had Longarm. "You're lookin' right pretty today."

"Thank you, Marshal." Emily looked slightly uncomfortable at the compliment, but she accepted it politely.

"If I didn't know that you don't have a husband, I'd say some man was mighty lucky to have you." Drummond shot a glance toward Longarm. "Unless Mr. Long here—"

"We're just business partners," Emily said. "I know that's a bit unusual, but still . . ."

Drummond shook his head. "It's none of my business, I know." He put his hat on again. "I'll let you folks get on with whatever it is you're doin'. I was just on my way in to see if Miz Hingerson has any breakfast left. That lady is one fine cook."

Longarm would have agreed with the marshal about that, but he didn't want to prolong the conversation. He didn't like Drummond. Maybe that was just instinctive because of the way Drummond looked at Emily with what seemed to Longarm like blatant lechery. Whether that was the case or not, Longarm didn't care. He wanted to get on up to Sweetwater Canyon and see what he could find.

Emily moved aside to let Drummond go past her on the walk that led to the porch. The marshal brushed against her as he passed, and to Longarm the contact seemed deliberate. He bit back his anger. He had more important things to worry about than a small-town lawman with a randy streak in him.

Emily stepped through the gate and handed Longarm his saddlebags. In a low voice, she said, "If I didn't know better, I'd say you were jealous, Custis." A smile twinkled in her eyes.

"Let's just go find that gold," Longarm muttered as he slung the saddlebags over the back of his horse and tied them on. He took the Winchester from Emily and slid it into the boot.

They rode out of Sweetwater City, following the creek again. They stayed on the north bank this time. The going was just as easy on that side. If they needed to cross over later, they could. The creek flowed fast, but it was shallow, only six or eight inches deep in most places, and from ten to twenty feet wide.

As the morning passed, they climbed higher into the foothills. At first, the canyon where the creek entered the mountains was not visible, but as the elevation rose they found themselves able to catch glimpses of their destination from time to time. Finally, in late morning, they reached a broad shoulder of land that jutted out from the base of the peaks. About two miles away, the dark mouth of the canyon was visible. Longarm's eyes narrowed as he reined in and studied it. Something about the canyon bothered him. If he had been the superstitious sort, he would have said that there was something evil and sinister about it, looming there like the maw of some great hungry creature, its jagged black walls like gigantic jaws waiting to snap shut on anyone foolish enough to venture between them. But since he wasn't superstitious, he put that thought out of his head. Tried to, anyway . . .

Emily didn't help matters by coming to a stop beside him and saying, "It's sort of a spooky looking place, isn't it?" She sounded nervous.

"Lots of basalt in those walls," Longarm said, trying to put things on a more practical basis. "That's what makes them so dark and jagged-looking. There are lava flows like that all over this part of the country. Reckon it took the creek a long time to carve out that canyon. Of course, the side of the mountain might've split from an earthquake or a volcanic eruption, and the creek just followed the course that was already there when the springs that feed it came to the surface."

"You sound like you know a lot about such things."

Longarm shrugged. "I've talked to a lot of geologists and professors and such-like over the years. Been around more'n my share of volcanoes, too. Of course, most of 'em was dormant, which is mighty lucky. You don't want to be around one of them varmints when it blows."

"I expect not," Emily said with a laugh.

Well, they had come this far, thought Longarm. They couldn't stop now. He heeled his horse into motion and said, "Let's go take a look." Emily rode alongside him.

They had gone less than a hundred yards, though, when several men came over the rim of the bench and galloped after them.

Longarm heard the rataplan of hoofbeats and hauled back on the reins with one hand while reaching for the Winchester with the other. He slid the rifle out of its sheath as he turned his horse to face the newcomers "Stay behind me," he told Emily, without being sure if she would actually do it. She edged her mount backward, and he was grateful for her caution.

The men riding toward them were strangers. Longarm had halfway expected them to be some of the same bunch that had confronted him and Emily the day before, but that wasn't the case. That didn't mean they weren't Diamond S riders, though. Didn't mean they were friendly, either, whether they rode for the Diamond S or not.

There were only four men in this party. One of them pushed ahead of the others and brought his horse to a halt first. He carried himself with an unmistakable air of being the boss. He looked to be of medium height as he sat his saddle glaring at Longarm and Emily. His face was craggy and weathered, and his hat was pushed back on a thatch of fading brown hair.

"You folks are trespassin'," he said curtly. "Who are you and what are you doin' on BMK range?"

Longarm suppressed the urge to laugh, even though he knew the situation was far from humorous. It was just so similar to what had happened the day before that the irony struck him. "I reckon you'd be Ben McKendrie, or one of his men?"

The man's glare twisted into a puzzled frown. "I'm McKendrie," he stated harshly. "Do I know you, mister?"

"No, but I know of you."

One of the other men snapped, "He must be one of the Dutchman's boys, Ben. Looks like a hired gun to me."

"Hired guns don't usually travel around with pretty gals like this one," McKendrie said. "I wouldn't put anything past Schermerhorn, though." To Longarm he said, "What about it, mister? You workin' for Axel Schermerhorn?"

"I'd never even heard of him—or you—until yesterday, McKendrie. And the lady and I don't want any part of the feud between you."

"You still ain't said who you are."

"Name's Custis Long. This is Miss Harrigan."

"What brings you up here?"

Longarm pointed to the dark defile ahead of them. "Just taking a look at Sweetwater Canyon."

McKendrie's puzzlement grew. "Why in blazes would anybody be interested in that place? It ain't good for a damned thing in the world."

"Maybe not, but we heard about it and wanted to take a look for ourselves."

Longarm could see McKendrie chewing that over, but before the rancher could come to a conclusion, one of his men warned, "Riders comin', Ben. Looks like the Dutchman and some of his boys."

Now Longarm had to swallow a curse. The last thing he and Emily needed was to be caught in the middle of a confrontation between two powerful ranchers who were ready to go to war against each other.

It looked like that was exactly what was about to happen, though. As Longarm hipped around in the saddle, he saw a small group of horsebackers heading toward them, led by the familiar stocky figure of Axel Schermerhorn.

Longarm looked for Dan Wilson, the Diamond S segundo, and was relieved when he recognized the man riding just behind Schermerhorn. If there was going to be a chance of heading off trouble, it would require Wilson's calming influence on his boss.

The sound of rifles being pulled from saddle boots made Longarm look around. McKendrie and his men held Winchesters in their hands now. "If that crazy old Dutchman wants a fight, by God we'll give him one!" McKendrie declared.

Emily looked anxiously at Longarm. He figured she was thinking the same thing he was. If he pulled out his badge and identified himself as a deputy United States marshal, even bitter enemies such as Schermerhorn and McKendrie might think twice about blazing away at each other. If it came down to the nub, that was what Longarm

110

would have to do. He wanted to wait until the last possible moment before revealing his identity, though, and he would just have to hope that he didn't cut it too close.

"Hold it right there, Schermerhorn!" McKendrie shouted. "Don't come any close unless you want a bullet welcome!"

Schermerhorn didn't rein in. He didn't even slow down. Instead, he yanked his hat off and used it to slap his horse's rump, urging the animal on to more speed. "You're on my range, you polecat!" he bellowed as he jammed his hat back on his head. "I'm gonna string you up like the no-good cow thief you are!"

Longarm got ready to jab his heels into his horse's flanks. If he had to move, it would have to be in a hurry. He figured he would grab Emily's reins and try to drag her out of the line of fire with him. First, though, he had to try to put a stop to this.

He started to reach for the pocket in his jacket where the leather folder containing his badge was stashed, but before he could complete the move, Dan Wilson galloped ahead of Schermerhorn and headed off the irate rancher. Schermerhorn was forced to draw rein or allow his horse to crash into Wilson's horse. The other two Diamond S riders came to a stop as well.

Wilson twisted his head around and shouted, "McKendrie, get back on your side of the creek, damn it! I won't be able to hold him back for long!"

One of McKendrie's men said worriedly, "We *are* on the north side of the creek, Ben. If there's any shooting, the law's liable to come in and say that we were in the wrong."

McKendrie grimaced. "Blast it! I don't like turnin' tail in front of that Dutchman." He looked at Longarm and Emily "I ain't through with you two, neither. But I reckon it'll have to wait until another day." With a motion that reeked of savage anger, he jammed his rifle back in its saddle sheath. His horse whinnied in pain as he jerked on the reins and hauled the animal's head around, sawing on the bit as he did so. He rode into the creek. His men followed him.

McKendrie didn't stop on the south bank of the stream. He kept going. Longarm didn't heave a sigh of relief until McKendrie and his men were at least a hundred yards away, though.

Schermerhorn cursed Wilson at the top of his lungs for interfering. The segundo took the abuse stoically, Longarm saw as he turned to look in that direction. "You can draw your damned pay, you traitor!" Schermerhorn concluded. He jerked his horse around almost as savagely as McKendrie had and raked it with his spurs. Schermerhorn galloped off, followed by his other two punchers.

Wilson shook his head slowly as he watched Schermerhorn ride away. Then he turned his horse and ambled over to where Longarm and Emily still sat on their mounts.

"You folks were sort of in the wrong place at the wrong time, as the old saying goes," Wilson greeted them as he reined in. He thumbed his hat back on his sandy hair.

"Obliged to you for getting in the way of that two-legged cyclone you work for," Longarm told him. "I reckon it cost you your job, though."

Wilson frowned and then shook his head. "You mean what Axel said about drawing my pay? Naw, he didn't mean it. He fires the whole blamed lot of us at least half a dozen times a month. Nobody can stay on his good side for very long at a time. But he don't stay mad at a fella for very long, either. I'll ride on back to the bunkhouse after a while, and there won't be anything more said about me drawing my pay . . . until next time, that is."

Emily said, "I don't see how you stand being treated like that."

"I've been with the boss for a long time," Wilson said

112

with a shrug. "It's amazing what you can learn to put up with." He paused, then went on, "Didn't expect to see you folks again so soon. Weren't you able to find Sweetwater City?"

"We found it, all right," Longarm replied, "but we rode back up here to have a look at that canyon. Noticed it yesterday and thought it looked interesting."

"That old place?" Wilson sounded as if he couldn't understand their interest. "It's just a canyon."

"But I'm studying geology," Emily said, "and it has some fascinating . . . formations."

Longarm hoped he kept the surprise off his face. They had been talking about geology and the composition of the canyon's walls a short time earlier, but nothing had been mentioned about Emily pretending to be a student. He had to admit that it sort of made sense, though. Emily was young enough to still be a student at some university. Longarm figured there probably weren't very many pretty young gals studying to be geologists, but such a thing wasn't impossible.

Wilson seemed to believe the story. He said, "Formations or not, I wouldn't go up there if I was you. The Indians who used to live in these parts said it was haunted."

"I'm not worried," Emily said. "I have Mr. Long here to look out for me."

Wilson shrugged. "It's none of my business." He pulled his hat down over his forehead again. "I'll mosey on now. The boss will have cooled off by the time I get back to the house. I'd watch out for that McKendrie if I was you." He grinned. "He ain't quite as levelheaded and slow to rile as the boss."

With that wry comment and a wave, Wilson turned his horse and loped off to the north, away from the creek. When he was gone, Emily said, "My goodness, Custis, I

113

thought we were going to find ourselves right in the middle of a battle."

"That's sure what it looked like for a few minutes," Longarm agreed. "Maybe now, though, Schermerhorn and McKendrie are through growling and snarling at each other like a couple of old dogs, at least for today. That gives us a chance to have a look-see around the canyon. Unless you'd rather go back to town and let me go on alone."

Emily laughed. "No chance of that, Custis. You're stuck with me, right to the bitter end."

Longarm grinned his acceptance of her declaration, but at the same time, he hoped that the end of this job wouldn't prove to be all that bitter.

Chapter 11

Even though the sun was shining, very little of the light seemed to make its way into the canyon, Longarm saw as they approached the opening. The defile seemed to swallow up the illumination somehow. The cliffs on either side of the canyon mouth were tall and sheer and almost as black as the walls inside. Longarm drew his Winchester as he and Emily rode between the towering ramparts. He thought holding the rifle might make him feel a little better, but he was wrong.

"I don't like this, Custis," Emily said in a hushed, nervous voice.

"Neither do I," he told her. "There ain't many things in this world, though, that can't be stopped by a 44-40 slug." He wished he really was as confident as he tried to sound.

The gloom of the canyon enveloped them as they rode on. There was enough light to see the creek flowing alongside the trail, but as Longarm looked ahead of them, things in the distance sort of faded out, like the world blurred and darkened and came to an end up yonder a ways. That made him feel even worse.

Here in this deep, dark canyon, the absence of light

meant that not much vegetation could survive. The grass on the creek banks died away. The horses' steel-shod hooves rang on bare rock. There were no trees, only a few hardy bushes growing here and there out of the stony faces of the canyon walls. On the south side of the creek, the bank dwindled away until the wall plunged sheer into the water. On the north side where Longarm and Emily rode, the trail was only about a dozen feet wide. Beside them, the creek narrowed, grew deeper and faster.

The place reminded Longarm, on a smaller scale, of the canyons along the Rio Grande, down in the Big Bend of Texas. He'd had a bad experience in one of those canyons a year or so earlier and nearly died there. The memory didn't bode well for what might happen here.

"If Floyd meant that the stolen gold was hidden in this canyon, I wish he had told you exactly where," Emily said. She kept her voice pitched quietly, but still the words echoed a little against the basalt walls looming above the two riders. Those walls also sent back echoes of the creek's bubbling and chuckling, playing like eerie music in the background.

"It was just a guess that was what Pollard meant," Longarm said. "A good guess, mind you, especially considering everything that happened before and after he pounded on my door. But maybe we were wrong." He turned his head to peer around them as they rode slowly through the canyon. "So far I ain't seen any place a fella could hide even one double eagle, let alone thousands of dollars' worth of them."

"How far into the mountains do you think this canyon goes?"

Longarm shook his head. "Can't tell yet. Several miles, anyway." He didn't relish the thought of being miles deep in the canyon, miles away from open air and sky. Tipping his head back, he looked up and saw that the canyon walls had risen to such towering heights that only a thin strip of blue was visible at the top. The air felt heavy, oppressive, like the air in a tomb that had been closed up for years, long years of decay and death.

They rode on in silence for a time. Longarm closely studied the trail ahead of them and the walls on both sides of the canyon. The walls were cracked and riven in places, the basalt forming tall, narrow columns. Some of the columns looked like they were ready to break off and topple into the canyon. If such a catastrophe ever occurred, Longarm pitied anybody unlucky enough to be caught in here at the time.

In other places, the canyon walls were pitted with holes, but the openings were so high, the rock faces beneath them so sheer, that no one could ever climb up to them. If Clete Harrigan had managed somehow to stash his loot in one of those holes, the gold would just have to stay there, because Longarm couldn't see any way of recovering it.

He paused once to look at an odd formation about forty feet up the opposite wall, a chunk of rock about the size of a bushel basket that formed a round, irregular shape. Another rock jutted out above it like the eaves of a house, and a thin column connected the top of the small boulder to the bottom of the shelf above it. Longarm wasn't quite sure how it remained suspended there. It seemed like the weight of the boulder should have broken that thin column of rock. Longarm knew, though, that nature was capable of many strange tricks. Things that didn't seem logical just *were*, and all a fella could do was accept them.

It was easy to lose track of time here in this world of shadows. It seemed to Longarm that he and Emily had been riding through the canyon for hours. He dug out his watch and opened the turnip. He had to bring the watch close to his face in order to read the position of the hands. They had actually been in the canyon a little less than an

117

hour. He shook his head in disbelief as he closed the watch and put it back in his pocket.

"I'm not sure how much longer I can stand this, Custis," Emily said. "I'm not trying to be a coward, but . . ."

"I know what you mean," Longarm agreed. "Maybe we ought to ride out of here, gather up a good supply of torches, and come back another time when we can bring our own light with us. Things might look a heap different in here if we could scare off some of them shadows."

Emily nodded. "That sounds good to—"

She stopped short as a new sound filled the canyon. It was a wailing moan, like that of a doomed soul in eternal torment. Emily stiffened in the saddle, eyes widening in terror. Longarm reached over and clasped her arm, holding it tightly as he saw the panic blossoming in her eyes.

"Hold on," he said, keeping his voice as calm as possible considering that his own nerves were jumping around like bacon in a skillet. "I reckon that's just the wind, blowing through some of those spires up on top of the canyon."

"Are . . . are you sure?" The moaning grew louder on the heels of Emily's question.

"No question about it," Longarm said, although he had questions yammering in the back of his brain like little imps. "I reckon it's time we got out of here, though."

Emily's head moved in a jerky nod. Clearly, she was more than ready to leave Sweetwater Canyon behind.

They turned their horses and started back along the trail they had followed into the canyon. Almost immediately, the volume of the moaning died down, and as they rode toward the canyon mouth, it dwindled away entirely. Longarm cast one more curious glance at the odd, beehive-shaped boulder as they rode past it, but he didn't slow down.

Now that they were leaving the canyon, time seemed to speed back up to its normal rate of passage. Longarm hadn't been aware of it slowing down until he checked his watch. Of course, that was all just a matter of perception, he told himself. The great river of time always flowed at the same speed, regardless of where a fella was or what he was doing. It was just the experiencing of it that seemed to change.

The canyon twisted and turned maddeningly. Longarm didn't remember all the bends in it. They had to have been there on the way in, though. The earth wasn't as changeless and immutable as some folks seemed to think, but a canyon didn't change its shape like a snake writhing back and forth in the dirt. Finally, the mouth of the canyon appeared in front of them, bright and beckoning like a door opening into paradise. Instinctively, Longarm and Emily both prodded their horses to a faster gait as they approached canyon's end. Longarm cast a glance over his shoulder. He wasn't sure why he did that, unless it was because a part of him wanted to make sure nothing had emerged from the shadows and might be gaining on them.

There was nothing back there, of course. Nothing but a plain ol' canyon carved out of stone. Still, Longarm felt a huge sense of relief when he and Emily emerged from the opening and warm sunlight washed over them.

They didn't stop until they were at least fifty yards away from the mouth of Sweetwater Canyon. Then they reined in and turned their mounts to look back at the opening. The water in the creek might be sweet, but there was nothing sweet about the canyon from which it flowed, thought Longarm. A shudder ran through him.

Emily's voice had a tremble of its own in it as she said, "That moaning . . . it was like a warning, Custis. It was telling us not to go any deeper into the canyon."

Longarm frowned. "I don't know about that. Like I said, it sounded to me like the wind—"

"The wind is still blowing. You can feel it for yourself. But as soon as we turned around and started out of the canyon, the moaning began to go away." Emily shook her head stubbornly. "It was a warning, I tell you."

"I'm not going to argue with you," Longarm told her. "That'd be just a waste of time and breath for both of us. I know one thing, though: I don't want you going back in there."

"*I* don't want to go back in there," Emily said with a shaky little laugh. "But I have to. We have to find that money, Custis."

"I'll find it if it's there to be found," he promised. "You've got my word on that. But there's nothing you can do to help me, no reason you have to come back."

"We'll see."

The way she said it told him that the argument wasn't over. But for now, he was willing to put it aside if she was. They turned their horses toward Sweetwater City.

They had ridden only a short distance, though, when Emily drew rein again. Longarm brought his horse to a halt and turned to look curiously at her. She pointed to some trees next to the creek and said, "Let's go over there."

"Why?" Longarm asked.

"I have my reasons."

He sensed that she wasn't trying to be coy. She just wasn't ready to explain herself yet. Longarm nodded, and together they rode over to the trees.

Emily dismounted and led her horse through the pines to a grassy clearing at the edge of the stream. Longarm followed her. When they got there, Emily tied her horse to a sapling and Longarm did likewise. Then Emily turned to him and said, "I need you to make love to me, Custis."

The same thought had occurred to Longarm. After the time they had spent in the canyon, in an atmosphere that seemed to reek of gloom and death, he felt the need to grab on to life and embrace it, and the best way he could think of to do that involved grabbing Emily and embracing her.

So that was exactly what he did, pulling her into his arms and bringing his mouth down on hers in a hot, urgent kiss.

Emily returned the kiss with just as much passion, her mouth opening so that her tongue could caress his mouth. Longarm's tongue darted around hers, circling it in a sensuous dance. She molded her body to his, her breasts flattening against his chest. He slid his hands down her back to her hips, cupping the denim-clad swells of flesh. She ground her pelvis into him. His shaft was rock-hard already. It prodded the softness of her belly through their clothes.

The kiss was long and sweet, but eventually it was overwhelmed by the need to get those clothes out of the way. Emily stepped back and unbuttoned her shirt. Longarm doffed his jacket and pulled his own shirt over his head. Emily threw her shirt aside and stood there beautifully nude from the waist up. Her breasts were firm globes of creamy flesh riding high and proud on her chest, the mounds topped by dark brown nipples that were already erect. The little buds of sensitive flesh hardened even more as Longarm looked at them. Emily arched her back a little and made a tiny pleading sound deep in her throat. Longarm stepped closer to her and lowered his head. He drew first one and then the other nipple into his mouth, sucking them gently and running the tip of his tongue around them as she stroked his head. He opened his lips wider and sucked as much of the soft female flesh into his mouth as he could. Emily sighed.

After a few minutes, still wearing her jeans and boots, she dropped to her knees in front of him and waited for him to take off his gunbelt and set it aside before she started unbuttoning his trousers. When she had them unfastened, she pulled them down over his hips, taking the long underwear with them. That freed his manhood, which sprang up into her face. Using both hands, she grasped the long, thick pole of male flesh and rubbed the velvety crown all over her face. She squeezed, milking a pearl-like bead of moisture from the organ's opening. Her tongue flicked out and lapped it up, drawing a shiver of pleasure from Longarm.

Leaning closer, Emily kissed up and down the length of his shaft as she reached between his legs to cup the heavy sacs suspended there. She bent lower to draw those sacs into her mouth, taking turns with them as Longarm had taken turns with her nipples. Then she raised her head a little, opened her mouth, and took the head of his manhood into her mouth. Her lips closed tightly, hotly, around it, and gradually she began to swallow more of him, filling the warm, wet cavern of her mouth with his hard, engorged flesh.

Emily spoke French about as well as any woman Longarm had ever encountered. It was a natural talent, too, nothing studied or artificial about it. As her oral caress boosted Longarm's arousal higher and higher, he felt it cleansing him as well, the goodness and trueness of what she was doing to him wiping out the dark shadows that had followed them from the canyon, clinging and coiling in their minds. That evil, if evil it was, was being blotted out by the pure delicious sensations now filling both of them. Longarm couldn't think of anything except the overwhelming climax boiling up inside him.

Even so, in the back of his mind an alarm sounded. He wanted to give Emily as much pleasure as she was giving him, and if she didn't stop what she was doing, pretty soon it was going to be too late for him to hold off. He started to say something, to warn her, but she stopped him by sucking harder and taking even more of his shaft into her mouth. Clearly, she wanted to bring him to culmination in this manner, and he was much too far gone to argue with her. He rested his hands on her head, tangling his fingers in her thick blond hair, and spread his feet a little wider to brace himself. At her urging, he flexed his hips, sliding his member back and forth between her tightly clenched lips. The sensation was incredible, so compelling that he had to exert every bit of his iron will to keep from thrusting so deeply into her mouth that she would gag. When his climax finally exploded from him, it seemed to come from the very core of his being. His shaft swelled even more and began gushing forth his seed in thick, scalding jets that filled her mouth.

Longarm's muscles felt weak, shaky, when he was finally drained. His heart pounded heavily in his chest and his pulse beat a mad tattoo inside his skull. Emily had swallowed every bit of what he had to give her, and she still cradled his softening member in her mouth. He stroked her hair for a moment as he caught his breath, then he stepped back and knelt in front of her, putting his hands on her shoulders. Gently, he urged her over onto her back.

She gave him a heavy-lidded smile as he stripped the rest of her clothes from her. When she was nude, he parted her legs, revealing the triangle of fine-spun blond hair and the pink folds it surmounted. He leaned over and returned the favor she had given him, licking and probing, thrusting his tongue into the core of her femininity, nipping at her insistent little bud with his teeth. She was wet already, and his skillful caresses sent her soaring into her first climax within mere moments. Longarm didn't stop there, though. He continued using his lips and tongue and fingers on her until her head and shoulders thrashed back and forth, her breasts heaved, and her fingers clawed at the ground on either side of her. She pushed her pelvis up into his face and cried out as her legs wrapped around his head. Soul-shaking tremors ran through her. And still Longarm gave her no respite. Again and again she climaxed until he was hard again and could kneel between her widespread thighs and ram his shaft into her, making her gasp and cry out yet again in inexpressible ecstasy as he emptied himself inside her one more time.

All in all, it was good, damned good.

But all good things, as they say, had to come to an end. Longarm slumped on top of her, trying to take most of the weight of his powerful, rangy form on his knees and elbows so that he wouldn't crush her. Their sweat-slick bodies rubbed together. Emily put her arms around him and hugged him so tightly he could barely breathe. Their lips brushed together in a feather-gentle kiss.

"Thank you," she whispered. "That was just what I needed."

"Me, too," Longarm agreed. Neither of them wanted to mention the reason they had needed the lovemaking. The memory of the pall cast over them by the canyon was still too fresh in their minds. Dwelling on it would wipe out all the benefits of what they had just done together. Better to concentrate on the moment and the pleasurable lassitude that washed over both of them as they lay there on the creek bank, snuggled in each other's arms.

Sooner or later, thought Longarm, they would have to get up, get dressed, and ride on back to Sweetwater City. Not just yet, though. No, not just yet . . .

Later, as he tightened the cinch on his horse's saddle, he looked over the animal's back to where Emily stood next to the stream, buttoning her shirt. At that moment he wished he were one of those painter fellas and could capture such a scene on canvas. But he didn't possess that skill, so he just looked at her instead and etched every detail that he could into his memory.

He had loosened the cinches and let the horses graze for a spell while he and Emily sat on the grassy bank and talked. Now the sun was beginning to lower toward the western peaks, and Longarm knew they needed to get started on their way back to the settlement. He was already dressed, so he got the horses ready to ride while Emily finished buttoning and straightening her clothes.

She glanced toward the mouth of the canyon. "I wish we didn't have to go back there," she said quietly.

"You don't have to," Longarm said. "It's my job, not yours."

"But it's my father who wanted to do one good thing while he still had the chance. And I owe him that chance. Anything I can do to help him fulfill it, I have to, Custis. Surely you can understand that."

Longarm just grunted. The way he saw it, Emily didn't owe Clete Harrigan much of anything. He had ignored her while she was growing up, and after her mother died he had stuck her in that academy back in Philadelphia so he wouldn't have to take responsibility for her. Sure, Harrigan might regret his crimes now, though Longarm wasn't fully convinced of that yet. But that didn't change anything. He was still a bank robber and a jailbird. Maybe such notions were uncharitable, thought Longarm, but that was the way he felt.

He wasn't going to say any of that to Emily, however. That would just hurt her needlessly. She could believe whatever she wanted to about her father. That didn't change Longarm's job one bit.

They mounted up and rode along the creek bank, skirting the trees. They had gone only a short distance when something caught Longarm's attention. It was a faint gleam off to the right on a small knoll, barely glimpsed from the corner of his eye. He said to Emily, "Hold on a minute," and turned his horse to ride over there.

"What is it?" she called after him.

"Just something I want to take a look at." His eyes narrowed. He had lost sight of whatever it was he had seen. He reined in and swung down from the saddle.

Walking slowly forward, his gaze searched the grass on the side of the knoll.

He spotted it again and crouched to reach down to the ground. His fingers found the item and picked it up, rolled it into the palm of his hand where he stared at it with a growing frown. It was a button, a small brass button. Not only that, but now he saw the pinched-out butts of several hand-rolled cigarettes. They were lying on the ground close to where he had found the button.

Turning his head, Longarm peered through the trees toward the creek. His eyes narrowed. From here he could see the stretch of bank where he and Emily had made love. The lurking suspicion in his head was confirmed.

Some son of a bitch had stood there calmly smoking quirlies and spying on them.

Chapter 12

"It was nothing," Longarm insisted. "I thought I saw something shiny over there, so I went to have a look. Just like an old magpie, I reckon. But I didn't find anything."

He hated lying to Emily, but he knew she would be mortified if he told her that someone had watched while they romped on the creek bank. The button he had found was in his pocket. If he ran into anybody missing an identical button off a vest or a jacket, he'd have a pretty good idea who the spy was. What he would do about it, though, was another question entirely. If folks got so carried away that they tore their clothes off and went at it outdoors, there sure as hell wasn't any law against anybody who happened to come along getting an eyeful of what they were doing. Considering the matter from that angle, you could almost say that the blame lay with him and Emily, not with the bastard who'd spied on them.

That didn't make Longarm feel any more kindly toward him, whoever he was.

"Are we going back up there tomorrow?" Emily asked as the canyon mouth fell out of sight behind them.

"I reckon, if you're bound and determined to go along."

With a smile, she said, "You ought to know by now,

Custis, that I'm always bound and determined about everything."

He couldn't suppress a chuckle. "I'm starting to get that idea, sure enough."

They rode on through the late afternoon. The light took on a reddish-gold tint as the sun neared the tops of the mountains to the west. Under these pleasant circumstances, Longarm could almost forget about the uncomfortable feelings that had run riot inside him while he and Emily were in Sweetwater Canyon.

Then, suddenly, something whipped past his ear, and the peaceful late afternoon was torn wide open by the spiteful crack of a rifle shot.

Acting instinctively, Longarm reached over and smacked a palm against the rump of Emily's horse. The chestnut leaped forward, startled by the slap, and broke into a hard gallop. The shot had come from somewhere to the right and behind them. The more distance between Emily and the bushwhacker, the less chance she would be hit by the next shot. And there *would* be another shot. Longarm was sure of that.

In a way, this wasn't a surprise. After all, it had been a couple of days since anybody had tried to kill him.

Longarm jabbed his heels into his horse's flanks and sent the buckskin lunging forward. Dirt and rocks exploded into the air a few feet to his right as another slug tore into the ground. He leaned forward in the saddle, making himself as small a target as possible against the horse's neck. A part of him hated to run away from a fight, but out in the open like this, that was his only option. If he could find some cover, a place where he could fort up . . .

Ahead of him, Emily still galloped along, trying to stay in the saddle and keep her horse under control. This sure as blazes wasn't like trotting around a Philadelphia park, thought Longarm. But so far she seemed to be doing a good job of it. She threw a glance over her shoulder at him, but she didn't slow down.

Longarm risked a look back, too. He saw a puff of smoke from a clump of boulders about halfway up one of the foothills. Another bullet whined past him, the high-pitched sound blending with the distant bark of the shot. Longarm urged the horse on. In another few moments he would be out of good shooting range, even for a Winchester.

But then, a second glance back showed him two men on horseback emerging from the boulders. They pounded after him, driving their mounts unmercifully.

Longarm looked in front of him again. If those bush-whacking bastards were going to chase him and Emily, it was more important than ever that he find a place to hole up and fight them off.

More shots crackled up ahead. Longarm bit back a curse as the real purpose of the ambush was revealed. The men behind them had just driven him and Emily into a trap.

Another pair of riders charged out of some trees. Six-guns barked as they rode toward Longarm and Emily. Longarm shouted, "Across the creek!" and waved an arm at Emily as she glanced back at him. Without hesitation, she veered her horse toward the stream. The bank was only about a foot tall along this stretch, so she had no problem sending her mount plunging into the water. Longarm was a few yards behind her as he did likewise. Water sprayed around them from the pounding hooves of the horses.

The broad shelf of land ran south from the creek. Most of it was open ground along here, with no place to hide, nothing to furnish any cover from bushwhackers' bullets. Longarm saw some trees up ahead, but they were at least a mile away. The men behind them who had rifles could pick them off easily before they reached the shelter of the pines.

They galloped the horses flat-out for a couple of minutes, putting as much distance between themselves and the gunmen as possible. Then, after checking the pursuit, Longarm shouted to Emily, "Head for the rim!" When she looked back at him in confusion, he waved toward the edge of the broad bench. Without hesitation, she did as he told her, swinging her mount in that direction.

The rim was less than half a mile away. They might make that, Longarm figured, after casting another glance over his shoulder at the men chasing them. The problem was that the gunmen now had a better angle at them, and the bullets searching for them began coming even closer. Twice, Longarm heard the lethal hum of slugs passing near his head.

But a miss, so they said, was as good as a mile. Grimly, he continued racing toward the slope where the bench dropped away into the more rugged foothills. He didn't bother drawing his gun and twisting around in the saddle to fire at the pursuers. At this range, and from the back of a galloping horse, he would just be wasting powder and lead.

Emily reached the edge first. She reined in and looked back at him nervously. Longarm motioned her on, but she didn't go. As he rode up, he saw why not. The ground dropped away steeply, and it was littered with rocks and brush and small, broken-down trees. Trying to ride a horse down that slope would be the next thing to suicide.

But staying where they were *would* be suicide, Longarm knew. They had only a couple of minutes at most before they would be shot out of their saddles.

"Grab on to the reins with one hand and the saddlehorn with the other," he told her. "Easy on the reins, though.

You'll be better off letting the horse pick his own way for the most part."

"But Custis, we can't . . . we can't go down that!"

"We ain't got any choice," he told her. "Come on!"

With that, he drove his heels into the buckskin's flanks and sent the horse over the rim.

The buckskin didn't want to go, either, but Longarm didn't give him a chance to crawfish. Almost before he or the horse knew what was happening, they were on their way down the slope, slipping and sliding and floundering. Dirt, rocks, and broken branches cascaded ahead of them. The horse let out a shrill, terrified sound as he tried desperately to keep his hooves under his body.

In this crazy, careening descent, Longarm didn't have time to do much of anything except struggle to maintain his seat. He was able to look over to the side, though, and he was glad to see that Emily had plunged down the slope as well. She and her horse were a short distance to Longarm's left and a little behind him. From the quick glimpse he got of her, he thought that she had her eyes closed as she hung on grimly to the saddle.

That wasn't such a bad idea, he thought. He kept his eyes open, though. He had always looked head-on at what life had to throw at him, and he was too old to change now. He let out a whoop of sheer excitement. This ride was scary as hell, but it was also damned exhilarating.

The thirty seconds or so that it took to reach the bottom seemed infinitely longer. A couple of times, Longarm's horse almost lost his balance and went over. Longarm was ready to kick his feet free of the stirrups and take his chances with a dive out of the saddle, but he knew he might not get that chance. He might be crushed, the horse rolling over on top of him, before he had time to make that move. But somehow, the buckskin stayed upright and continued sliding and lunging toward the bottom. When he finally got there and stumbled out onto more level ground, for a second Longarm didn't even realize what had happened. Then a surge of triumph went through him and he turned to see Emily's horse shaking itself as dirt and rocks showered down around him and his human burden. Emily was hunched over in the saddle, holding on to the horn for dear life, her eyes still clenched tight shut.

"You're down!" Longarm shouted at her, breaking through the cocoon of sheer terror that engulfed her. "Come on! We've gotta get out of here!"

They still weren't out of danger, despite the daredevil, breakneck ride down the slope. The men who were after them could come down the same way, but it was more likely they would stay up there on the rim and take pot-shots at them. Already Longarm had spotted a thick stand of pines no more than two hundred yards away. If he and Emily could reach those trees in time, they would be safe. It wasn't long until night, and they could hide in the trees until darkness fell.

With a shake of her head that mirrored what her horse was doing, Emily opened her eyes and looked around. Longarm leaned over and snatched the reins out of her hands. "Come on!" he said again. He put the buckskin into a run and dragged Emily's chestnut after him.

He didn't hear any shots from the rim, but he knew he might not be able to hear them over the pounding of the horses' hooves. Both animals were winded, but they responded gallantly when Longarm called on them for one last dash. They raced through gathering shadows toward the welcoming shelter of the trees. Moments later, barely slowing, Longarm and Emily rode into the pines. Gloom enshrouded them. He reined to a halt and swung down from the saddle. As Emily stopped beside him, he stuffed her reins back into her hands and reached for the Winchester jutting up from the saddle boot. Snagging the rifle, he pulled it free and put his back to the trunk of one of the trees at the edge of the growth, peering around it toward the shoulder of higher ground where they had been ambushed.

Longarm saw movement up there in the fading light. A couple of men rode along the rim, rifles in hand as they peered down the slope. He might have been able to pick off one of them, but he held his fire. If the bushwhackers weren't sure where he and Emily had gone, he sure as hell didn't want to announce their location with a chancy shot. Those gunmen had to know that their quarry probably had fled into the trees. They would know, as well, that if they continued the search, they would likely be riding right into Longarm's gunsights.

He wasn't surprised when they turned and rode away, moving back from the rim and out of sight. His enemies had made yet another attempt on his life, and again they had failed. The difference was that this time, he hadn't been able to hurt them, either.

"What will we do, Custis?" Emily asked from behind him.

"Wait here until it's good and dark," he said. "Then we'll try to find our way back to Sweetwater City."

"What about those men?"

"I think they've given up . . . for now," he told her. His hands tightened on the Winchester. "But we'll keep our eyes open, just in case they decide to try again."

That was one thing they could count on, he thought maybe not tonight, but sooner or later, the men who wanted them dead *would* try again.

Both of them were bone-tired as they rode into Sweetwater City. Full night had fallen quite a while earlier, and finding their way back to the trail that would take them to the settlement hadn't been easy. Longarm had ridden the whole way with the Winchester across the saddle in front of him, just in case he needed to use it in a hurry.

They hadn't run into any trouble, though, and now as

they rode toward Mrs. Hingerson's house, Longarm didn't think their enemies would try to bushwhack them right here in the middle of town. Nothing was impossible, though, so he kept his eyes open and all his other senses alert.

As they came up to Mrs. Hingerson's place, the front door opened and a man stepped out onto the porch, carrying his hat in one hand. He turned to say something to someone just inside the door, then put his hat on and came down the walk. Stopping at the gate, he looked up at Longarm and Emily as they reined their mounts to a halt.

"Well, well," Marshal Jace Drummond said. "I was just thinking about sending out a search party to look for you folks. Miz Hingerson got a mite worried when you never came back from your little outing today. Are the two of you all right?"

"Just fine," Longarm said. He swung down from the saddle and turned to take the reins from Emily as she dismounted as well. "I reckon we got a little lost."

"Is that so? Miz Hingerson says you're horse buyers? I never heard of folks getting lost looking for horses to buy . . .'specially in a place where there ain't no horses for sale, as far as I know."

Longarm bristled at the suspicion in the local lawman's voice, but he suppressed the reaction. His voice was calm and cool as he said, "Miss Harrigan and I like to look around the country, whether we find any horses to buy or not."

"Well, I reckon I can understand that." Drummond chuckled. "I like taking long rides in the country with a pretty gal, too."

Drummond started past them, but Longarm stopped him by reaching out and putting a hand on his arm. He turned Drummond so that the light from the house's windows fell on the front of his body.

Angrily, Drummond jerked free of Longarm's grip.

134

"What the hell!" he exclaimed. His hand moved toward the butt of his gun. "Damn it, Long, didn't anybody ever tell you it ain't very smart to go around manhandling lawmen like that? You're lucky I didn't pistol-whip you, or worse, put a bullet in you!"

"Sorry," Longarm said. "Thought I saw a bat swooping down at your head."

"A bat! There're no bats around here. Closest critters like that are down in the southeast part of the territory, around that big old cave!"

"My mistake," Longarm said.

Drummond grunted. He walked away, casting a final irritated glance over his shoulder at Longarm.

Emily leaned closer and asked in a half-whisper, "What was that all about, Custis? I know you didn't see a bat!"

"I reckon not," Longarm admitted. "I just don't like Drummond much. Figured I'd hoo-raw him a little."

"Like he said, that wasn't a very smart thing to do. I'd think you would want to cooperate with the local authorities. I know he sounded pretty suspicious of us, but you could have taken care of that by showing him—"

Longarm held up a hand to stop her before she mentioned his badge and his true identity as a federal lawman. Even though whoever was behind the continuing attempts on his life almost had to know that he was a deputy U.S marshal, Longarm had a feeling there might be more than one set of enemies around here. Those other adversaries probably weren't aware that he was a star packer for Uncle Sam.

"Drummond said Mrs. Hingerson was worried about us," he said. "Go on in and set her mind at ease."

He led the horses around to the stable while Emily went into the house. After unsaddling the animals, rubbing them down, and seeing that they had water and grain, Longarm went to the rear door of the house and pulled it open. He heard voices from the parlor and followed them.

Emily and Mrs. Hingerson sat on the divan. The land-lady was saying, "—thought you'd both fallen in a ravine or something. I'm certainly glad to see that you're all right." She looked up at Longarm and added, "I was just telling Miss Harrigan how concerned I was about the two of you, Mr. Long. Why, just before you got here, I was pestering Jace—I mean, Marshal Drummond—about riding out to search for you."

From the way she said the marshal's name, Longarm got the feeling there might be a bit of a romance between her and Drummond. He didn't know if that was a good idea or not, since he didn't like Drummond, but that really wasn't any of his business.

He took his hat off and said, "Sorry we worried you, ma'am."

"Well, there's still some supper warming on the stove." Mrs. Hingerson stood up and straightened the apron she wore over her dress. "I'll go dish some up for you."

"That'd be mighty nice of you," Longarm told her with a grin. "It's been so long since I've eaten that my belly's starting to wonder if my head's still attached to my shoulders."

"Mine, too," Emily said.

After they had eaten, Emily insisted on helping Mrs. Hingerson clean up. Longarm went into the parlor, stood in front of the fireplace, and lit a cheroot, tossing the lucifer into the ashes when he was done with it. He stood there smoking for a few moments and blew a couple of almost perfect smoke rings. Then he clenched his teeth on the cheroot and slid his hand into his pocket. His fingers closed on the brass button and pulled it out. He stood there looking down at the little circle of metal lying on his palm.

He had been acting purely on a hunch when he grabbed hold of Drummond and turned the lawman around so that the light fell on the front of his clothes. But that hunch had paid off. As soon as he'd seen the button lying on the ground, Longarm had thought there was something familiar about it and that he might have seen buttons similar to it in the recent past. Tonight that impression had been confirmed. The vest worn by Marshal Jace Drummond sported buttons that were identical to the one Longarm now held in his hand.

And one of the buttons on Drummond's vest was missing. The marshal of Sweetwater City was the man who had spied on Longarm and Emily as they made love.

Chapter 13

Given everything that had happened, not being able to sneak into Emily's room that night and spend some time in bed with her wasn't as difficult as Longarm might have anticipated. They had been through a great deal, they had survived several attempts on their lives, and a peaceful night's sleep would be good for both of them. Longarm's slumber was deep and dreamless, and he awoke the next morning feeling refreshed.

Except for the nagging feeling in the back of his mind that he had seen or heard something important, something that might prove to be the key to locating the loot Clete Harrigan had hidden in Sweetwater Canyon years earlier. But whatever it was, Longarm couldn't pin it down. He had experienced such hunches before, on other cases, and they always drove him half loco until he finally figured out what was bothering him.

So far in his career, he had always managed to come up with the answers he needed. But there could always be a first time for failure . . .

Breakfast was just as good as it had been the day before. When they were finished, Longarm and Emily went into the parlor, and Emily asked quietly, "Are we going back up there today?" She didn't need to specify where she was talking about.

Longarm nodded. "I'm convinced that money's up there. If it wasn't, somebody wouldn't be trying to stop us from finding it." He kept his voice pitched so low that only Emily could hear him.

"I don't understand," she said with a frown. "If whoever's been trying to have us killed knows my father hid the loot in the canyon, why don't they just go and get it?"

Longarm had pondered that very question, and he was convinced he knew the answer. "Because all they know is that the gold is somewhere in the canyon. They haven't found it yet, either, but they don't want to risk any competition from us. That's why they keep sending bushwhackers after us."

Slowly, Emily nodded. "That makes sense. So if we ride up there again, we're risking another attempt on our lives?"

"That's right," Longarm told her. "Would it do any good to ask you—"

She was shaking her head before he could even finish asking the question. "No, it wouldn't do any good at all. I'm going with you, Custis."

For a moment, he considered taking her up to her room, gagging her, and hog-tying her. He figured that was the only way he could prevent her from returning to Sweetwater Canyon with him. But knowing how resourceful she was, as she had demonstrated on more than one occasion in the past week, he decided she would probably get loose somehow and come after him anyway.

"I'll go tend to the horses," he said. "Be ready to ride in ten minutes."

"I will be," Emily promised with a grin.

After saddling the horses, Longarm poked around in the stable and found some pieces of old lumber and a discarded horse blanket. He ripped the blanket in strips and bound them around the ends of the boards. They would do for torches, though it would have been better if he could have soaked the fabric in coal oil or something like that. He tied the torches together with a piece of twine, then used another piece to lash them to his saddle. This time when he and Emily penetrated the gloom of Sweetwater Canyon, the torches would furnish some illumination. He found a coil of rope in the stable as well, an old lasso left behind by some cowboy, and hung that over the saddlehorn. It might come in handy.

Emily came out onto the porch as Longarm led the horses around front. He glanced up and down the street, halfway expecting to see Marshal Jace Drummond skulking somewhere nearby. He didn't see any sign of the local lawman, though.

Emily was carrying a single-shot rifle. Longarm frowned at the weapon and asked, "Where'd you get that?"

"I borrowed it from Mrs. Hingerson. She said it belonged to her late husband. I told her that we'd spotted a mountain lion yesterday and thought it would be a good idea if we had an extra rifle along."

That was actually a pretty reasonable explanation, thought Longarm. And if they ran into trouble again—as certainly seemed possible, even probable—having more firepower could definitely be a good thing.

"Smart idea," he told her. He held the rifle while she mounted, then passed it up to her. "You can rest it across the saddle in front of you. Just don't drop it. Guns are touchy. Sometimes they go off when they get dropped."

"I'll remember that," Emily promised.

Longarm swung up into the saddle and led the way out of Sweetwater City. His eyes flicked from side to side. Still no Drummond. But if the marshal was planning to follow them and spy on them again today, he wouldn't be obvious about it. Maybe he was just a damn voyeur, thought Longarm, remembering the French word. It was possible, though, that Drummond could be up to something more than spying on folks. Longarm intended to keep a close eye on their back trail today.

He was pretty familiar with this foothill country by now, so it didn't take as long to reach the broad bench onto which Sweetwater Canyon opened as it had the previous day. They were there by midday. That was a good time to be venturing into the canyon, Longarm knew. With the sun almost directly overhead, more light would penetrate into the declivity. They might not even need the torches.

As they rode between the towering basalt walls, Longarm listened for the keening wail that had filled the canyon on their previous trip. He didn't hear anything unusual, and since the wind wasn't blowing very hard today, he was more convinced than ever that that was what had caused the wailing.

"It's still gloomy in here," Emily commented, "but it's not as bad as yesterday. I don't feel like a ghost is going to jump out at me at any second."

"I don't reckon there are any ghosts up here," Longarm said.

Emily laughed. "You sound serious, Custis. Do you really believe in ghosts?"

"Well, I'll tell you," Longarm replied slowly. "I've seen a few things in my time that were a mite strange. Things I couldn't really explain. Most of the time I consider myself a pretty hardheaded old son, but every now and then I run across something that's just, well, strange. There's a line from an old hymn that says further along we'll know more about it. Reckon that's the way I feel about ghosts and such-like."

"There are depths undreamed of in you, Custis Long."

"I might not go so far as to say *that*," he responded with a grin.

Despite the sunlight slanting into the canyon, there were still patches of deep shadow. Longarm felt a chill go through him when he rode through some of them. He tried to keep track of the twists and turns the canyon made, but after a while that grew hopeless. It was a good thing there weren't any smaller canyons branching off of this one. If there had been, getting lost would have been mighty easy.

The clinking of horseshoes on the rocky path echoed back from the canyon walls. Longarm listened closely as they rode, hoping that if anyone were following them, he would be able to pick out the sound of their horse's hooves. As far as he could tell, nobody was back there behind them.

They rode past the oddly shaped rock formation that reminded Longarm of a beehive. The day before, they hadn't gone much farther than this. Soon, they would be penetrating deeper into the canyon than ever before. The sun was trending toward the west now, too, which meant it was growing gloomier inside the canyon. Well, they had the torches if they needed them, he told himself.

"Where would my father hide that money?" Emily mused, addressing the question as much to herself as to Longarm. "What sort of hiding place would catch his eye? It would have to be some place he could find again without much trouble . . ."

Suddenly, Longarm stiffened in the saddle. He hauled back on the buckskin's reins. "Wait a minute," he said, motioning for Emily to stop. That nagging feeling in the back of his mind had returned, stronger than ever. He had seen something important, and not long ago, either . . .

The Hornet's Nest.

The phrase popped into his brain. According to Emily, Clete Harrigan had taken part in the series of futile Confederate charges against Ulysses S. Grant's Yankee soldiers who were dug in behind a wooden fence near the old church known as Shiloh. One of the Rebels who'd been fortunate enough to survive those suicidal attacks had staggered back to his lines and exclaimed, "It's like a hornet's nest in there!" The name had stuck, and ever since, that part of the famous battle had been known as the Hornet's Nest. Of course, there hadn't been a real hornet's nest there, or even anything that looked like one; the name had come from the way bullets filled the air like angry hornets.

Still, Clete Harrigan had considered that an important moment in his life. A defining moment, according to Emily. And back up the canyon a little ways was a rock formation that looked like an actual hornet's nest more than anything else. Longarm had thought of it as a beehive, but that was subtly wrong, he realized now.

It looked like a hornet's nest. He was sure of it!

And that didn't have to mean a damned thing. It might be just coincidence.

It might not be, though. He lifted the reins and turned his horse, backing the buckskin carefully on the narrow trail. "Let's go back a ways," he told Emily. "I want to take a look at something."

"What is it, Custis?" Excitement crept into her voice. "Have you figured out something?"

"Maybe. We can find out pretty quick-like."

Emily turned her horse and followed him. They rode back along the creek, following the twists and turns of the canyon. As they did, the shadows grew thicker. Longarm didn't know if clouds had drifted across the sun or if the gloom was increasing because the hour was growing later. Whatever the cause, he was glad now that he had brought along the torches.

A short time later, they reached the spot where the rock formation was located. Longarm reined in and looked up at it, hanging there on the side of the sheer wall some forty feet up on the opposite side of the creek. Was that a shadow on the wall behind it, he asked himself with a surge of eagerness, or something else? An opening of some sort, maybe?

The next question was: how in the blazes was he going to get up there?

There was only one way he could see. He looked down at the coil of rope hanging around his saddlehorn.

"What is it, Custis?" Emily asked. "What's up there on that cliff?"

Longarm pointed. "See that round chunk of rock just sort of hanging there?"

"Yes. What about it?"

"Notice anything unusual about it?"

Emily frowned. "Well, I'm no expert on rock formations . . . I've never seen anything quite like it, though. It looks like it ought to break off and fall."

"Yeah, but it hasn't so far. I've run across all sorts of balancing rocks and such-like, things that don't hardly seem possible, but nature keeps coming up with them anyway. There's something about that rock, though . . ." Longarm wanted to see if she recognized the same thing he did without him telling her . . . or if his imagination was just stretching itself too far. "What's it look like to you?"

"It looks like . . . a hornet's nest." Her voice took on a hushed quality as the words came out. She lifted a hand to her mouth. "My God, Custis! You don't think my father saw that and was reminded of . . . of that battle at Shiloh . . ."

"You said that was mighty important to him. Maybe he saw that rock, and what's behind it, and took it as an omen of some sort. A sign that he'd found the right hiding place for that loot."

"What do you mean, what's behind it?" Emily shook her head in confusion "I don't see anything."

"I think there's a little cave up there," Longarm said.

"Like the ones we saw farther up the canyon. The mouth of it is pretty much hidden by that rock, though, and what you can see blends in because the canyon wall is so dark."

"I don't know," Emily said dubiously. "I'm not convinced there's an opening up there, and even if there is, how could anybody get to it?"

"Only one way." Longarm lifted the coil of rope from his saddlehorn and hung his hat in its place. "Climb hand over hand."

Emily's eyes widened in disbelief "Oh, no," she said "You can't, Custis. Nobody could do that."

"You'd be surprised what a fella can do if he wants to bad enough." Longarm shook out a loop, his fingers moving with practiced skill. Back in his cowboying days, he had been a fair hand with a rope, though there had always been men better with a lariat than he was, on every spread where he had worked. He tried to estimate how long this lasso was. Sixty feet was a standard length, and that was what he judged this one to be. He looked it over, searching for weak spots or places where rats might have gnawed on it while it was lying around in the stable behind Mrs. Hingerson's house. The rope was old, but he decided it was in pretty good shape. He would just have to hope it was good enough.

"I still don't see how you're going to do this," Emily said.

Longarm pointed. "See where that rock juts out above the Hornet's Nest? If I can dab a loop on it, it ought to hold me. Then I can swing across the creek and go up the wall." He pulled a pair of gloves from his saddlebags and drew them on. He would need the protection of the sturdy leather for his hands. When he had dismounted, he pulled one of the makeshift torches from the bundle and stuck it behind his belt. It was going to be awkward up there, trying to light a torch while still hanging on to the rope, but he would do the best he could. Assuming he found a cave behind that rock, which was far from a sure thing.

Emily got down from her horse and held the reins of both animals as Longarm stood on the edge of the trail and slowly swung the loop over his head. He kept his eyes fastened on the slab of rock that protruded above the Hornet's Nest. His arm moved faster, and the twirling rope picked up speed as well. Suddenly, with a flick of his wrist, Longarm made his first cast.

The throw missed, falling short of its mark. Longarm had expected that. He pulled the rope in quickly, not wanting it to fall in the creek and get wet. A wet rope would be even heavier, and casting a loop so far up was hard enough to start with. He gathered in the lasso, set himself, and tried again. This time the throw was far enough but just off to the side. He grimaced. His arm was getting tired already. With his jaw clenched tightly, he concentrated, swung the loop faster and faster until it was little more than a blur, and finally threw it for the third time.

The rope sailed up into the air, the loop opening wide, and settled down over the jutting rock.

Emily clapped her hands. She had been watching anxiously. "You did it, Custis!" she enthused. "But are you sure you can climb that far?"

"Well, if I don't, I reckon I'll get a good dunking when I land in the creek," he said with a grin. He wasn't feeling as happy-go-lucky as he sounded, though. The creek was deeper here, but not deep enough so that he could survive a fall from that height. Memories of plummeting through that Big Bend canyon and plunging into the Rio Grande flashed through his mind. Surviving that fall had been little short of a miracle; he had to wonder sometimes just how many such miracles were still coming to him. By any reasonable measuring stick, he had more than used up his share already.

Still, there was no other way to do this. He leaned and

tugged on the rope, testing it. The loop was secure over
the rock, and the rope seemed strong enough. He backed
up a few feet to get a running start, then lunged toward
the creek. With a yell, he launched himself into the air.
His hands gripped the rope tightly.

Longarm's weight and momentum made him swing out
over the water, toward the rock wall on the far side. His
trajectory sent him toward the surface of the creek. He
pulled up his booted feet to clear it and then thrust them
out in front of him to absorb the shock of hitting the
canyon wall. He felt the impact shiver all the way up his
legs, but he was able to hang on. He bounced off, then
swung against the wall again. This time he managed to
brace the soles of his boots solidly against the basalt,
which was a little slippery to start with and was made
more so by the spray that sometimes came up from the
fast-flowing stream.

"Custis, are you all right?" Emily called.

"Yeah," he grated, hoping the terseness of his answer
would convey to her the message that he didn't have any
strength to waste on idle conversation. Most of his weight
was on his arms, and already they ached from the strain.
He looked for better footholds and shifted his feet a little.
That took some of the burden off his arms. He set himself,
reached up, and pulled.

His progress up the rope was maddeningly slow. He
had to pause and search for places to put his feet each
time he got ready to climb higher. He had heard of folks
who climbed rocks like this for the fun of it. Longarm
didn't see the appeal, himself.

After what seemed like an hour, he was only ten feet
up the rope, a fourth of the way to the Hornet's Nest. The
gloom in the canyon thickened around him. Stubbornly,
he kept climbing. From time to time, Emily called out
encouragement to him. He began to fall into a routine,
which helped in a way. But he grew more tired with each

foot that he climbed. His pace remained about the same.

But then he was at the halfway point, and he knew he could make it. A few more heaves on the rope and he was closer to the Hornet's Nest than he was to the ground. So now it was easier to go on up, he told himself. Just keep climbing.

The wall became more jagged, less sheer. That helped. There were more and better footholds. He felt his optimism surging. Thirty feet now, and still going. The muscles in his arms quivered, but only a little. His hands ached, but he could stand that. He braced his feet and pulled himself up another six inches.

He wasn't sure he had reached the Hornet's Nest until he bumped his head on the bottom of it.

Now he could see that he had been right. There *was* an opening behind the odd-shaped rock. He shifted his weight to the left and swung that way, being careful not to rub the rope too much over the rough surface of the Hornet's Nest. He didn't want it to fray now. Longarm got his feet set and took a turn of the rope around his left wrist for extra support. With his right hand, he twisted the piece of lumber behind his belt so that it stuck out in front of him. Then he reached inside his shirt pocket, found a lucifer, and brought it out. A flick of his thumbnail set the match afire. He held the tiny flame to the wad of old horse blanket at the end of the makeshift torch and hoped it would light.

It did. The flame caught and spread, and in a moment the blanket was burning brightly. Longarm leaned forward, bringing the torch closer to the opening in the canyon wall. It was a shallow cave no more than five feet deep, with a mouth about a yard on each side, forming an irregular square.

And inside the cave was a neat stack of oilcloth-wrapped packages. Longarm had no doubt they contained the gold coins stolen in Clete Harrigan's final robbery.

148

From the looks of the dust that lay on them, they had not been touched since Harrigan placed them there more than five years earlier. Caching the loot up here must have been one hell of a job, he thought as he felt a mixture of relief and excitement surge through him. Gold was heavy. Harrigan probably hadn't been able to carry more than one package with him at a time, which meant he had made this arduous climb—Longarm counted the bundles—ten times.

He turned his head and called down to Emily, "It's here!"

"What?"

"The money!" Longarm said "It's here!"

She clasped her hands together in front of her face. "Thank goodness."

The torch was going out. Longarm didn't need it anymore. He pulled the board from behind his belt and let it fall into the creek. Now that he had located the loot, it was time to reveal who he really was and round up some help in Sweetwater City. He wanted to get a block and tackle and rig a pulley up here so that the money could be recovered without anyone having to climb up and down every time. He would send a wire to Billy Vail, too, and let the chief marshal know about the discovery.

Getting down was a lot easier than going up. Longarm kicked off from the wall and slid down the rope as he swung back in each time. The gloves kept his hands from blistering as the rope moved through them. When he was close to the creek, he gathered up the end of the lasso and tossed it over to Emily. "Tie it around the buckskin's saddlehorn," Longarm told her, "and then back him up until the rope's good and tight."

She followed his instructions. Longarm hoped the horse was good at standing still. He worked his way across to the trail, his feet dangling above the water. When he finally dropped onto solid ground again, a shudder went through him The effort required for the ascent had worn him out.

"We'll find a nice heavy chunk of rock and tie the rope to it so we can leave it here," he said. "That way we won't have to throw a loop over that slab up there when we come back."

"How are we going to get the gold down?"

"I'll deputize some fellas and bring them out from the settlement," Longarm explained "We'll rig up a pulley—"

He stopped short as he heard the rattle of hoofbeats on the rocky trail. Somebody was riding up the canyon.

And the way things had been going recently, that was almost guaranteed to mean trouble.

Chapter 14

Longarm's plan to leave the rope in place had to be aban-
doned. The lasso pointed straight to the hiding place of
the stolen gold. Until he knew who the approaching riders
were, he couldn't afford to reveal the cache. Quickly, he
untied the rope from the saddlehorn and with a flick of
his wrist loosened it on the other end. Another flick sent
it sliding free from the jutting slab of rock. The rope
dropped into the creek. Longarm let it go so that it sank
and was carried away by the current. Now that he knew
where the loot was, he could always get another rope before he came back to recover the money.

The riders had almost reached the nearest bend in the
canyon. As Emily watched him worriedly, Longarm
pulled his Winchester from the saddle boot. "Better have
that rifle you borrowed ready," he told her grimly. "No
telling what's about to happen, but chances are it won't
be good."

Two men rode around the bend. They were moving
quickly but not carelessly on the narrow trail. At the sight
of Longarm and Emily standing there with rifles in their
hands, the men reined to a halt. Longarm knew one of
them right away, and the other one looked familiar.

A grin spread across Dan Wilson's friendly face as he thumbed back his hat. "Seems like I keep running into you folks," he said. "This is sort of an odd place to do it, though."

Longarm relaxed slightly at the sight of Axel Schermerhorn's foreman. He was pretty sure the other rider was one of the Diamond S punchers; he knew he had seen the man recently and associated the memory with the encounters he and Emily had had with the fiery-tempered Dutchman.

"Reckon you must be studyin' rock formations or something like that," Wilson went on.

"Something like that," Longarm agreed.

"Well, there are all sorts of odd rocks in this canyon." Wilson's grin faded a little. "You folks aren't really horse buyers, are you? You're after something else up here."

Now that he had located Harrigan's cache, Longarm knew he could reveal that he was a lawman and stomp out the fuse that was burning on the impending range war between Schermerhorn and Ben McKendrie. At the very least, he ought to be able to use his authority as a federal lawman to keep Schermerhorn and McKendrie on their best behavior for a while. Long enough to recover that stolen loot up in the cave behind the Hornet's Nest, anyway.

He was about to pull out his badge and admit who he really was, when instinct made an alarm bell clamor in the back of his brain. Something was wrong here, and even though Longarm wasn't sure what it was, he sensed that it could be deadly. Instead of answering Wilson's question, he said, "Maybe you ought to tell me what you're doing up here."

The Diamond S segundo's grin was completely gone now. Wilson wore a frown instead. "Why the devil would I do that? Anyway, my boss claims all the range on this side of the valley up to the mountains, including this canyon. I've got a right to be here. You don't."

Longarm couldn't argue with that without telling Wilson that he was a lawman. As Longarm hesitated, letting several seconds tick by, he looked over at the other rider, studying the lean, dark face, the hawk nose, the pitted cheeks, the low-slung gun . . .

Suddenly, he knew what was wrong. He had seen the second man a couple of days before, sure enough, when Schermerhorn and McKendrie angrily confronted each other beside Sweetwater Creek.

But this man had been with McKendrie's cowboys, not Schermerhorn's Diamond S punchers. Longarm was sure of that. Why was he riding with Wilson now?

The only answer was a double-cross.

Wilson must have seen the flare of understanding in Longarm's eyes. The foreman's hand stabbed toward his pistol, and he yelled, "Take him, but don't hurt the girl!"

Longarm brought the Winchester up even as Wilson shouted the order. He fired first. Wilson hauled back on his horse's reins as he drew, causing the animal to rear. Longarm's shot missed, whipping past Wilson's head and racketing on down the canyon.

"Emily, get back!" Longarm snapped as he worked the rifle's lever. The other man had his pistol out now, and both he and Wilson tried to bring their weapons to bear as Longarm darted between the horses, using them for cover.

Colts banged, and Longarm's buckskin whinnied shrilly as a bullet burned its flank. From somewhere behind him, Emily's rifle blasted as she joined in the fight. Her gun was a single-shot, which meant she would have to reload before firing again. Longarm straightened from his crouch and fired over the back of the chestnut, spraying three shots toward Wilson and the other man as fast as he could work the Winchester's lever. He didn't hit anything except the rock walls of the canyon, but the lead flying around their heads made Wilson and the other man haul their horses around and head for the nearest cover. That was the bend in the canyon about fifty yards away.

Longarm sent a couple of shots after them to hurry them on their way. He knew, though, that they would rein in as soon as they were out of sight. They still blocked the way out of the canyon.

"Stay behind the horses," Longarm said over his shoulder to Emily as he kept the Winchester trained on the spot where the two men had galloped around the bend.

"Custis, what happened? I thought Mr. Wilson was one of the few people we could trust around here!"

"So did I," Longarm admitted. "But if there's one thing I've learned, it's that things ain't always what they seem to be." He paused. "Got that rifle reloaded yet?"

"Yes, it's ready—" she began.

"Long!" The shout came from around the bend, interrupting Emily. "Long, you hear me?"

Longarm could easily make out Wilson's voice over the sound of the creek "I hear you!" he called. "What the hell do you want?"

"There's no need for us to be shooting at each other! What's going on between the Dutchman and McKendrie is no business of yours! What's it matter to you that I'm taking McKendrie's money, too?"

"He's working for McKendrie?" Emily asked in a half-whisper. "I thought he was the foreman of the Diamond S."

"He is," Longarm said grimly. "But as soon as I realized that fella with him is one of McKendrie's men, I knew somebody had to be double-crossing somebody else. Either Wilson or the other gent had to working against the man who's supposed to be his boss. Now we know which one it is."

"Wilson's the traitor," Emily said. "But he's right, Custis. That's none of our business. Isn't the trouble between the two ranches a matter for the local law?"

She was right, of course, thought Longarm. Wilson might be money-grubbing scum, but there was no federal statute against that, or else half the politicians in the country would be behind bars.

"How about it, Long?" Wilson shouted. "Put up your guns and ride out of this canyon, and we'll all forget about what happened here today!"

It was a tempting offer, but every instinct in Longarm's body cried out for him not to trust Wilson. He had already been wrong about the man once; a second such mistake might prove to be deadly.

He turned and motioned to Emily. "Grab the horses and take them on up the canyon!" he hissed. "Be as quiet about it as you can. I'll stall Wilson."

"Do you think if we agree to his offer, he'll double-cross us, too?" she asked.

"A scorpion stings," Longarm said "It's in his nature."

Emily nodded, understanding what he meant. She gathered up the reins.

"Long!" Wilson shouted again. "I'm gettin' a mite impatient!"

"Hold your horses!" Longarm bellowed back at him, raising his voice even more than before so that echoes bounced back from the canyon walls. With that going on, there wasn't much chance that Wilson and his partner would hear Emily leading the horses away. "How do I know we can trust you?"

"Hell, if I really wanted you dead, I wouldn't have headed off trouble with Schermerhorn twice! I could've let the Dutchman have you!"

Longarm twisted his head to look over his shoulder. Emily had the horses moving briskly along the trail now. He glanced up at the Hornet's Nest. Wilson hadn't seemed interested in that at all. He just didn't want Longarm and Emily revealing his treachery to Schermerhorn.

The surest way of shutting them up, though, would be to kill them, weight down their bodies with rocks, and dump them in the creek. Their bones would be washed clean and might stay here in this gloomy canyon forever. Longarm couldn't take a chance on that. He started slipping backward along the trail, keeping his eyes and the Winchester trained on the bend.

"Long! Damn it, Long, I'm gettin' mad now!"

Emily was around the next bend with the horses. Longarm turned and broke into a cat-footed run after them, trying to be quiet.

"Long!" Wilson hollered one more time. Then, a moment later, hoofbeats sounded. Wilson must have figured out that Longarm and Emily were trying to slip away, and now he and his companion were taking up the chase.

Longarm stopped at the next bend and lined his sights on the spot where Wilson and the other man would appear. As soon as they came barreling around the bulge of rock, Longarm triggered off two shots. That made the horses dance skittishly toward the edge of the creek. Wilson and his companion struggled to bring the animals under control. Longarm's rifle blasted again, and the second man yelled in pain as the bullet tore through the flesh of his upper arm. Wilson grabbed the reins of the other horse as the wounded man sagged in the saddle. He hustled back around the bend, leading the horse.

Longarm had drawn first blood. Maybe Wilson and the other man would give up. He didn't really believe that would happen, but there was a chance, anyway. He turned and ran after Emily and their horses, not bothering now to try to be quiet.

Ahead of him, Emily slowed a little, but Longarm motioned for her to go on as fast as she could. His long legs enabled him to catch up in a matter of minutes. "Mount up!" he called to her as he approached. "Head on up the canyon!"

Emily hit the saddle and urged the chestnut into a fast lope. Longarm caught up with the buckskin a moment later and made a running mount, grabbing the saddlehorn and hauling himself up into leather. He thundered along behind Emily.

They hurried through the stretch of canyon where the walls were pocked with caves. All of the dark openings were too high to reach, otherwise Longarm might have considered forting up in one of them. All he and Emily could do was press on and hope that they would find a place they could defend against their two pursuers.

A bullet whined past Longarm's head. He threw a look back over his shoulder and saw Wilson and the other man riding after them. The second man was lagging a little, no doubt in pain because of his wound, but he hadn't given up. Neither had Wilson. The Diamond S segundo guided his mount with his knees and used his hands to fire the carbine he held. Basalt chips sprayed from the canyon wall near Longarm as a slug struck it.

To his dismay, Longarm saw that the trail beside the creek narrowed even more up ahead. It was barely eight feet wide where Emily rode, and to someone on the back of a galloping horse, that seemed mighty narrow indeed. There was little room for error. A misstep by the horse, a leaning too far one way or the other in the saddle by the rider, almost anything could send both of them plunging over the edge into the cold, fast-flowing creek. The steadily growing gloom in the canyon didn't help matters. The half-dark made accurate shooting more difficult, but it could also cause one of those deadly missteps.

Longarm reined in and twisted around in the hull to throw lead at Wilson and the other man. Orange flame geysered from the muzzle of the Winchester. Wilson and his companion didn't even slow down.

"Custis!" Emily called urgently.

Longarm jerked around and banged his heels against

the buckskin's flanks. The horse lunged ahead. Longarm couldn't see Emily, and after a second he realized why. The canyon took another of those sharp turnings. He had to slow down to make it safely around the bend. A bullet spanged off the canyon wall near him as he did.

Longarm hauled back on the buckskin's reins as he spotted Emily waiting for him up ahead. Beyond her, the trail dwindled even more. It was perhaps a yard wide as it hung over the brawling creek. It started to climb, too, at a fairly steep slope. Eventually, the trail might lead out of the canyon. Or it might peter out entirely. There was no way to know which without climbing it.

A sure-footed mount could make it, thought Longarm, if the rider could take it slow and easy. Even better would be for the rider to dismount and lead the horse up the trail. But if he and Emily did that, they would be easy pickings for Wilson and the other man.

Emily's only chance was for Longarm to keep the two pursuers from reaching this point.

"Go on," Longarm told her as he swung down from the saddle. He stepped up beside the chestnut and tied the reins to the saddlehorn. "Get down and lead your horse up the trail. Mine will follow."

"But what are you going to do, Custis?"

"Stay right here and deal with Wilson and that other fella. I'll follow you on up there later."

Emily's voice was shaky as she said, "You mean you'll sacrifice your life for mine."

"I ain't of a mind to sacrifice anything," Longarm declared. "Like I said, I intend to stop those old boys. And you'll be taking a chance, too, never you worry about that. We don't know where this trail goes. You could wind up in a bigger fix than me."

"Custis, are you sure—"

"Go on," Longarm told her firmly but gently. "Just take it slow and careful going up that trail."

She took a deep breath. "All right." Already they could both hear the hoofbeats of the other horses approaching. Quickly, Emily leaned toward him and brought her mouth up to his in a brief, passionate kiss. "You be careful, too, Custis," she urged.

A grin flashed across his face. "Get going now."

She jerked her head in a nod and started up the narrow trail, holding tightly to the chestnut's reins. The horse followed, and the buckskin fell in line behind.

Longarm went to the bend in the canyon and thrust the barrel of the Winchester around it. He leaned out and saw Wilson and the other man hustling their horses along the trail, some forty feet away. Wilson's carbine barked at the same time as Longarm's Winchester. Longarm ducked back as rock chips stung his face. He didn't know if he'd hit anything or not.

He heard the horses stop. A moment later, the hoofbeats started again, slower and more deliberate now. He risked a glance around the bend. Wilson and the other man had dismounted and were driving their horses up the trail in front of them at a walk. Longarm bit back a curse. With the horses for cover, he couldn't get a good shot at either of his enemies.

Wilson might have some knowledge of this canyon; Longarm didn't know about that. If Wilson was aware that the trail grew so narrow here, he would know that Longarm and Emily couldn't move fast anymore. He could afford to take his time closing in on them.

Longarm's only option was to kill the horses, block the trail, and force Wilson and the other man to clamber over the dead animals and come after him on foot. He hated to think of shooting down innocent horses.

He didn't get the chance to, because the next second, with a whoop and a pistol shot, Wilson sent the horses stampeding up the trail toward Longarm. Wilson was using the animals as living weapons now. Longarm grimaced and turned to run up the trail. He had to get a little breathing room so he could deal with this new threat.

The horses barreled around the turn, coming dangerously close to the edge of the trail. Wilson and the other man raced along right behind them. As slugs sang around his ears, Longarm turned and dropped to one knee, bringing the Winchester to his shoulder. He fired at the onrushing horses. One of the animals screamed in pain and veered unsteadily toward the creek. Its hooves slid off the edge, and with a shrill, terrified whinny, it twisted and fell into the water with a huge splash. Longarm fired again and thought he saw the second man go spinning off his feet, but then the other horse was practically on top of him and he had to throw himself aside desperately to avoid being trampled. Even so, a hoof clipped his hip and knocked him hard against the canyon wall. The Winchester slipped out of his hands to clatter on the rocks at his feet. Longarm reached for his Colt, only to have Wilson shout, "Hold it, Long!"

Half off his feet, braced awkwardly against the canyon wall, Longarm stood there motionless as Wilson stalked toward him, carbine leveled. Longarm knew that if his hand moved an inch toward the butt of his revolver, Wilson would fire. At this range, the man couldn't miss.

"You put up one hell of a fight, Long," Wilson said, panting a little from the exertion. "Before I kill you, I'd sure like to know who you really are and what you're doing up here."

"I don't much care what you want, old son," Longarm said. "Far as I'm concerned, I reckon you can go to blazes." The longer he talked, the better chance Emily had of getting away. *If* there was a way out of the canyon at the end of this trail . . .

"I might've let you go, you know. Probably not, but I might have. Now that you've killed Marlon, though, I reckon I can't. McKendrie wouldn't like that."

"Why'd you go to work for him, anyway?" Longarm asked, stalling to give Emily more time. "I thought you rode for Schermerhorn's brand."

"I did, for a lot of years." Bitterness crept into Wilson's voice. "You got any idea what it's like to work for a crazy man and put up with his bullshit all the time, year after year after year? Worst part of it, that Dutchman's only crazy about half the time. The rest of it is just pure meanness on his part. Sure, when McKendrie asked me to work for him on the sly, I said yes. It's no more than Schermerhorn deserves."

"So you're helping McKendrie stir up trouble in hopes that he'll run Schermerhorn out of these parts?"

"Or kill him," Wilson said bluntly. "The funny part of it is, the whole thing's got something to do with this canyon. That's why I figured you and the girl weren't telling the truth about why you were up here. Satisfy my curiosity before you die, Long ... what's up here that's so all-fired important to McKendrie?"

The question made Longarm's brain whirl. Ever since coming to this part of the territory and learning of the friction between Schermerhorn and McKendrie, he had assumed it was nothing but a typical clash between powerful, greedy ranchers, land hogs who always wanted more than they had and didn't need a good reason for their greed. Now Wilson was making it sound like there was some deeper motive for the feud, at least on McKendrie's part.

"Are you saying that McKendrie doesn't want all of the Dutchman's range, just this canyon?"

"That's right," Wilson said "Even offered to buy it from him, right at the first. But Schermerhorn wouldn't hear of it, of course, and the fact that McKendrie wanted it just made him more determined than ever to hang on to it. When McKendrie filed on it and the rest of the range, Schermerhorn went crazier than usual. Even hired a lawyer down in Santa Fe to fight McKendrie's claim in court. They've got it all tied up down there now, no telling when the legal part of it will be hashed out." Wilson's voice sharpened with suspicion. "Are you tellin' me you didn't know any of this, Long?"

"It's news to me," Longarm admitted.

The barrel of Wilson's carbine dipped a little. "Then who the hell are you, and why are you here?"

Longarm might have told the truth. Even with everything that had happened, Wilson might be persuaded to back down if he knew that he was threatening a federal lawman. Besides, a new theory had begun to spin crazy circles inside Longarm's brain, a theory that would answer some, but not all, of the questions that Wilson's revelations had raised.

But Longarm didn't have a chance to say anything else, because at that instant, Wilson grunted and the distant crack of a rifle sounded, both at the same time. The impact of a bullet flung Wilson against the canyon wall and made him drop his carbine. He rebounded from the basalt face and pitched to the trail, lying motionless as a dark puddle spread around his head. Somebody had drilled him from long range. Judging by the sound of the shot, the bullet had come from up on the canyon rim, on the far side from the trail. In this bad light, it had been either one hell of a good shot, or one hell of a lucky one.

And for all Longarm knew, he was next.

Chapter 15

He threw himself to the ground, snatching up the Winchester as he rolled over to the base of the wall and pressed himself to the black rock, making himself as difficult a target as he could in the fading light. No more shots came, though, after the one that had killed Dan Wilson.

Long minutes crept by. The darkness in the canyon deepened. When Longarm was convinced that no one on the rim could possibly see him, he climbed to his feet and went over to Wilson. Though he was fairly sure that the treacherous segundo was dead, he dropped to a knee and searched for a pulse in Wilson's neck. After a moment, Longarm straightened. Wilson would never betray anyone else.

Longarm tipped his head back to stare up at the strip of sky high overhead. It was a deep blue, retaining just a hint of daylight but already dark enough so that a few stars were beginning to appear. Soon, a perfectly stygian blackness would fill the canyon.

And with that utterly apt sense of timing often displayed by the cosmos, the wind picked up at that moment and the eerie wailing once more drifted through the shadows, sounding to Longarm like the cry of a departing soul. Dan Wilson's soul, maybe . . .

Time to go.

With a little shake of his head, he broke out of the grim reverie that gripped him and started up the trail, leaving the other horse to find its own way back out of the canyon. Emily had to have heard the shots and would be wondering what had happened to him. The sooner he caught up to her, the sooner he could set her mind at ease.

In the thickening shadows, he couldn't move too fast without risking a fall. He followed the trail up the canyon. It rose higher and higher above the water, and Longarm was convinced that sooner or later it would bring him to the rim. The canyon itself narrowed until it looked like he could have jumped to the other side. He knew that appearances were deceptive, however. More than a dozen feet still separated the two walls of the canyon.

The drop-off to his right became dizzying as the trail climbed higher. Longarm's hip ached where the horse had hit him. The steepness of the slope took a toll on him as well. He wasn't as young as he used to be, he mused. He had spent years packing a star for Uncle Sam, flirting with danger and cheating death. How much longer could he keep that up? He told himself that it was just the gloom of the canyon and the dissonant keening of the wind that made him think such bleak thoughts, but he recognized that there was some truth in what he was feeling. No one lived forever, especially a man in such a dangerous line of work. Most men could take comfort in the knowledge that there was at least a chance they would die in bed, surrounded by their loved ones. But not him, thought Longarm. When his time came, he would die in a dark, bitter, lonely place like this one, an outlaw's bullet in his guts, tormented by regrets for the things he had done . . . and the things he had not done . . .

He stopped short and shook his head again. He found

a cheroot in his pocket and stuck it in his mouth, clenching his teeth on it and leaving it unlit. "You can die some other time, old son," he told himself aloud. "Right now you got things to do." He started up the trail again, his natural confidence coming back into his stride.

He thought about calling out to Emily, but the knowledge that someone else was lurking around this canyon kept him silent. He had no idea who had shot Wilson. Whoever it was, they might be an ally . . . or they might not. Longarm couldn't take that chance.

Surely he would reach the top of the trail soon, he told himself. He had been climbing for what seemed like hours; and now he was making his way by touch, keeping his left hand on the canyon wall while he searched in front of him with each foot in turn, making sure of where he was stepping before he put his weight down there. The need to be so cautious slowed him down even more.

But after an eternity, he sensed space opening around him and looked up for the first time in quite a while. Now he could see a much broader swath of the night sky, glittering with stars almost from horizon to horizon. A few more steps and he was there, out of the canyon, the trail ending in a boulder-strewn shoulder of fairly level ground with a mountain peak soaring above it. Longarm stumbled a little from weariness as he stepped away from the canyon. Where was Emily? He knew she must have made it this far, because she hadn't been down below on the trail.

That was when several dark shapes moved out from behind the big rocks, and a harsh voice said, "Don't move, Marshal. I've had such a hard time killin' you that now I'd like to make it last a while." The words were accompanied by a round of metallic clicking that Longarm recognized as the sound of several six-guns being cocked.

He stood stock-still, making no movements that might spook his captors into shooting. The spokesman had referred to him as a marshal. That meant he had to be aware

165

of Longarm's true identity. And that fit right in with the idea that had come to him earlier.

"Take it easy, McKendrie," he said. "Or maybe I ought to call you Rainey. That's your real name, ain't it, old son? Matt Rainey, right bower to Clete Harrigan?"

Ben McKendrie strode forward, keeping his gun trained on Longarm. Up here in the moonlight and starlight, Longarm had no trouble recognizing the owner of the BMK ranch. Before becoming a cattleman, though, McKendrie had had another career, that of bank robber. Longarm was sure of it.

"You've figured out too much, Long," McKendrie grated. "Of course, it don't really matter whether you know who I am or not. You'll die anyway. I've been tryin' to have you killed ever since I got word from Leavenworth that Clete was sending a message to you by way of that old cellmate of his."

"You had friends on the inside of the prison," Longarm said, weaving together in his own mind the strands of fate that had brought them to this high, lonely, barren spot. "You knew Harrigan's daughter had been visiting him. Hell, maybe you even knew that she'd been trying to convince him to reveal where he hid the loot from that last job."

"The loot that he cheated me out of!" McKendrie—or Matt Rainey—said. "All I got was a few hundred dollars' worth of those double eagles. Clete hid the rest. I always figured the money was somewhere in this canyon. These were his old stomping grounds, and he told me more than once that he knew every foot of Sweetwater Canyon. But I've been lookin' for nigh on to five years without findin' it!"

"I can see why you'd get a mite nervous to have somebody else poking around, especially a lawman."

"Damn right," McKendrie grated. "I tried to silence Pollard before he ever got to you, but my boys were too

166

late. Then, when you started down here, and with Clete's daughter to boot, I knew you had to be after the gold. Well, by God, I'm not givin' it up! I've got it comin' to me."

"You've got something coming to you, all right," Longarm muttered "I ain't sure it's hidden loot, though."

McKendrie snarled a curse. "Put that rifle on the ground and then drop your gunbelt, Long. I'm gonna enjoy killin' you."

Carefully, Longarm bent over and placed the Winchester on the ground at his feet. As he started to unbuckle the cross-draw rig strapped around his hips, he said, "Maybe you better think twice about killing me, McKendrie. Could be I know where that gold is."

"If you know, so does the girl. Since I've got her, I don't need you."

Longarm's jaw tightened in anger. He had been wondering what had happened to Emily. As soon as he recognized McKendrie, he had figured that it was likely the outlaw had captured her as soon as she reached the top of the trail out of Sweetwater Canyon. Now McKendrie had confirmed that.

Without taking his gaze off Longarm, McKendrie called to his men, "Bring out the girl!"

A couple of men emerged from behind one of the boulders. They had Emily between them, each of them holding tightly to one of her arms. She was struggling against their cruel grips, but she stopped fighting as soon as she saw Longarm. "Custis!" she exclaimed. "I hoped they wouldn't get you, too."

McKendrie gave a humorless chuckle. "You see, Long, I don't need you at all. But I would like to know what happened to Wilson and Marlon. When we spotted you and the girl riding into the canyon again today, I sent them after you while the rest of us took the long way up here."

Longarm hesitated before answering. McKendrie

wouldn't have had any reason to kill Wilson. Wilson worked for him, and besides, the Diamond S segundo hadn't known anything about McKendrie's true identity or what he was really after. Wilson had proven that by the questions he'd asked Longarm. McKendrie's other men knew the truth, but the outlaw had deliberately kept Wilson in the dark, letting him think that he was just selling out Schermerhorn in a range war.

So whoever had shot Wilson was a new player taking cards in this game and a potential ally for Longarm. Longarm didn't want McKendrie to find out about that just yet.

"They're back down in the canyon, dead," he finally said. That was true enough. If McKendrie wanted to assume that Longarm had killed both of them, so much the better.

"I'll have to get the bodies and make it look like they killed each other," McKendrie said, thinking out loud. "I'll blame it on Wilson, and that'll give me the excuse I need to wipe out that crazy Dutchman once and for all. Then I can search this canyon from one end to the other without havin' to worry about Schermerhorn and his riders tryin' to stop me."

Longarm laughed, not bothering to conceal his scorn. "What makes you think you'll find Harrigan's cache even if Schermerhorn's not around to dispute your claim to the canyon? Hell, you said yourself you've been searching for years without finding it."

McKendrie came a step closer, and his voice trembled with rage as he said, "I'll find it, damn you! All I need is some more time." He leered. "Time to work on that girl and get her to tell me what she knows."

Time was what Longarm needed, too. Time for that mysterious rifleman who had killed Wilson to show up and take cards in this hand . . .

A cold wind whistled across the mountainside, and the wailing from the canyon grew louder. So loud, in fact, that Longarm almost didn't hear the sudden flurry of shots. But he saw one of the men holding Emily suddenly fly backward, driven off his feet by a bullet. The other man staggered, letting go of her to clasp his arms across his belly where he'd just been shot.

"Emily! Down!" Longarm shouted as he dived for the rifle at his feet. McKendrie's revolver exploded at the same instant, Colt flame blooming in the starlit night. The slug slapped through the air where Longarm had been a heartbeat earlier.

His hands closed on the Winchester. Lying on his belly, he angled the barrel up and pulled the trigger. The bullet ripped into McKendrie's body, traveling upward at a steep slant. Its impact drove him up on the toes of his boots. He swayed there for a second, then pitched forward on his face.

McKendrie wasn't the only enemy Longarm had up here, though. Several of his men were still on their feet. They opened fire, flinging lead toward the big lawman. He rolled over, levering the Winchester as he did so, and snapped a shot into the midst of the outlaws as they scattered for cover. One man went tumbling head over heels, brought down by Longarm's shot. Longarm pushed up on hands and knees and scrambled a few feet before throwing himself down behind a rock. It didn't offer much cover, but it was better than nothing.

A few yards away, Emily bent over and snatched a revolver from its holster on the hip of the first man who had been shot. He lay motionless in death, while his gutshot partner writhed and screamed nearby. Emily whirled and triggered a couple of shots toward the rest of the gang, then dropped behind a rock as Longarm had done.

They were outnumbered, but they were both armed now. And they weren't alone, either, thought Longarm. The hombre who had opened the ball by shooting Emily's

169

captors was still out there somewhere in the dark. As if to prove that, gun flame lanced down from the higher ground to the right, directed at the rest of McKendrie's men. Bullets whined around wildly in the rocks, ricocheting with deadly effectiveness. One man popped up to return the fire, but before he could squeeze off a shot, Longarm drilled him through the head, sending his hat spinning into the air. The Stetson hit the ground a second after its now-dead owner did.

Emily held her fire. She was waiting for a good shot, Longarm decided. She got it a moment later, the Colt in her hand blasting as one of the BMK gunmen tried to dart from one boulder to another. He went over backward like he'd been punched in the chest by a giant fist.

Caught between three fires, the men knew they were in a bad spot. They tried to bust out, firing wildly as they made a dash for their horses, which had been left a short distance along the slope. Longarm came up on his knees and pumped shot after shot from the Winchester until the magazine was empty. Emily emptied the revolver, and a volley came from their unknown ally up the slope as well. One by one, McKendrie's men fell, scythed off their feet by the hail of lead. The last one pitched forward on his face just before he reached the now nervously milling horses.

Longarm set the empty rifle aside and picked up the gunbelt he had taken off earlier at McKendrie's command. He strapped the rig back on and drew the Colt. Moving in an alert crouch, he walked toward the sprawled gunmen, keeping the revolver trained on them all the time. None of McKendrie's men moved, however. Even the one who had been screaming and rolling around earlier was still and quiet now, either dead or unconscious.

When he had finished checking on the fallen men, Longarm lowered the Colt to his side but didn't holster it. He called to Emily, "You can come out now. They're all dead." He turned his head to look up the slope. "You, too, mister, whoever you are."

Emily stood up and hurried over to Longarm. She put her arms around his waist and hugged him tightly as she pressed her head against his broad chest. "I was so scared, Custis," she whispered. "I thought they were going to kill both of us."

"Might have if we hadn't gotten some help." Longarm's keen eyes spotted the dark figure working its way down the slope toward them. "Much obliged, mister," he said as the man reached relatively level ground and started toward them. He carried a rifle slanted across his body.

The starlight reached the man's face, and Longarm recognized Marshal Jace Drummond. "A mite out of your jurisdiction, ain't you, Marshal?" Longarm asked. "Not that I'm complaining."

"Under the circumstances, I didn't figure you'd mind me taking a hand, Marshal," Drummond said. "That's what McKendrie called you, ain't it, Long? Marshal? You a federal lawman or something like that?"

"Deputy United States marshal out of Denver," Longarm confirmed.

"And you're after some sort of outlaw loot hidden down in Sweetwater Canyon?"

"An army payroll stolen over five years ago." Longarm didn't add that the robbery had been masterminded and carried out by Emily's father. Drummond might know that already if he had been eavesdropping while McKendrie was gloating.

Drummond let out a low whistle. "Must be a hell of a lot of money."

"I reckon," Longarm said "You might get a reward for helping us recover it." Considering everything that had happened, he was willing to forget about the way Drummond had spied on him and Emily as they made love by the creek.

171

Drummond shifted the rifle in his hands so that it pointed toward Longarm "Or I might just take me the whole thing—and this girl here."

Longarm stiffened and felt Emily tense against him. "You son of a bitch," he grated, jaw clenched tight in anger. "Don't that badge on your vest mean anything to you?"

"It means that I'm expected to risk my life to protect a bunch of skinflint townies who won't pay a man a living wage," Drummond said bitterly. "Well, I'm tired of that, Long. It's time I got my hands on a decent payoff."

"I was right about you," Longarm said. "I never did like you."

Drummond laughed harshly. "Oh, now I'm gonna lose a heap of sleep over *that!* I don't care what some dead federal star packer thinks of me, and that's what you're gonna be in a few minutes."

Emily still huddled against Longarm. Her hands moved like she was too nervous to keep them still. "I won't go with you," she said to Drummond. "You'll have to kill me, too, and then you'll never know where that money is."

"You'll go with me, all right," Drummond said confidently. "If I have to knock you out and hog-tie you, you'll go with me. And I know where there's an old cabin I can put you. We'll have us a fine old time until you decide to go ahead and tell me where to find that loot. I've been wantin' a piece of you ever since the first time I saw you."

Emily shuddered and then lifted her head to look up into Longarm's face. "I'm sorry, Custis," she said. "I . . . I have to do what he says."

"Do what you have to," he told her in a voice like stone.

Drummond laughed again. "Step away from him, gal, so we can get this over with."

Emily moved back and away, turning as she stepped

172

toward Drummond. Her arm came up, the gun in her hand rock-steady as she leveled it at the local lawman. "Drop your rifle, Marshal, or I'll kill you," she said.

Drummond flinched a little, startled by the unexpected threat. But then he relaxed, and in the starlight, his face creased in an ugly grin. "Oh, now, you just bought yourself even more trouble. I know there's no bullets in that gun. You emptied it at McKendrie's men a few minutes ago."

"I'm not bluffing, Marshal," Emily said.

"I'm goin' to take particular pleasure in makin' you talk. Makin' you scream is more like it," Drummond said. He started to bring his rifle up. "Soon as I kill this federal lawdog—"

Emily shot him in the head.

The Colt in her hand bucked as fire lanced from its muzzle. The bullet slammed into the middle of Drummond's face and drove him backward off his feet. He was dead before he hit the ground.

Emily dropped the gun and put her hands to her face as reaction hit her. Longarm stepped forward and kicked the fallen rifle well away from Drummond, even though he was sure the treacherous lawman was no longer a threat. Then he put his arms around Emily and held her tightly.

"You did just fine," he told her. "I knew I could count on you."

She fought back sobs. "If I . . . if I hadn't been able to get a cartridge from your belt and slip it into that gun . . . if I had missed . . ."

"You didn't," Longarm told her. "You did what you had to do, just like I said."

She looked up at him "You knew what I was doing?"

"I figured it out in time to play along with you," he said with a nod. He looked past her at Drummond's sprawled shape. "It's a damned shame whenever a lawman goes bad. Reckon we do owe him a debt of thanks, though. He saved my bacon when Wilson was about to shoot me down in the canyon, and then up here we probably wouldn't have been able to turn the tables on McKendrie if Drummond hadn't helped us."

"He didn't have to turn out to be evil," Emily said.

Longarm looked up at the stars and listened to the wailing of the wind. "Some folks just can't seem to help it," he said. "It's in their nature, just like the scorpion."

Chapter 16

Emily closed her fingers around Longarm's erect organ and slowly moved them up and down. The already stiff rod swelled and hardened even more.

"You like that, don't you?" she asked with a mischievous smile.

"What man wouldn't?" Longarm said.

"I don't really know. I haven't done this to all that many men." She leaned over and licked at the lobe of his ear. In a whisper, she asked, "Would you like to hear about it?"

"Maybe later," Longarm growled. He rolled toward her, poised for a second between her widespread thighs, and then drove his shaft into her, filling her warm, clasping sheath.

They were in Emily's room in Mrs. Hingerson's house in Sweetwater City. The landlady's prohibition against such behavior had been forgotten in the uproar that had seized the town in the past twenty-four hours. The town marshal was dead, along with an influential local rancher and more than half a dozen of his men, as well as the foreman of the other big cattle spread in the area. And ten oilcloth-wrapped bundles containing a fortune in gold coins now reposed in the vault of Sweetwater City's only bank, guarded around the clock by deputies Longarm had sworn in. Several of the deputies were Axel Schermerhorn's men. The Dutchman seemed to have been shocked back into sanity by the news that his segundo had been betraying him. It seemed that Schermerhorn had looked on Dan Wilson as something like a son, despite the abuse that Schermerhorn had heaped on his head. Maybe that was just the way the Dutchman thought things were supposed to be. Whatever the case, he was now cooperating with Longarm and had promised to help keep the money safe until an army paymaster and a military guard detail could arrive to claim it. Longarm planned to remain on hand, too, even though he didn't expect any more trouble.

He figured he might as well spend some of that time pleasantly, though, which was why he was in Emily's room, in Emily's bed, in Emily. His hips pumped in the timeless rhythm, the beat that lifted both of them higher and higher until their climaxes took them and they shuddered together in release.

With them still joined, Longarm rolled onto his back, taking her with him. She rested atop him, her head pillowed on his chest. He stroked the short blond hair and said, "That was mighty fine. Makes me feel alive again."

"Me, too," Emily said. "When I was back in Philadelphia, I never dreamed that the world could be such an exciting place. And so dangerous, too."

"They seem to go together more'n I'd like. But we take what life throws at us, I reckon, and do the best we can."

She leaned over and kissed him. "I'm glad life threw you at me, Custis Long."

His shaft, softer now but still semi-erect, slipped out of her. She reached down to fondle it. "The first time I touched this and realized how big it was, I knew I had to have it inside me sooner or later. Does that make me a shameless hussy?"

Longarm chuckled. "Maybe a mite. You're talking about that first night in camp, on the other side of the Sangre de Cristos?"

"No, silly. During the stagecoach ride."

With a frown, Longarm lifted his head. "Wait just a dang minute. You mean to tell me you were *awake* all that time?"

"Of course I was."

"I thought you were asleep!"

"I know. I figured as much. But I didn't see any harm in letting you think that. That way you wouldn't think I was *too* shameless."

Longarm couldn't stop the laughter from bubbling up inside him. He tightened his arms around her and kissed the top of her head. "You are a piece of work, Emily Harrigan!" he told her. "Damned if you ain't!"

Later, after she had fallen asleep, Longarm slipped out of bed and pulled his clothes on in the dark. Slumber should have claimed him by now, too, but for some reason he was still awake. He had snatched only a brief hour of sleep in the past twenty-four. The rest of the time had been spent getting Emily back to Sweetwater City and rounding up a posse to go with him back to the canyon. That had taken all of the previous night. The following day had been spent supervising the removal of the various bodies back to the settlement, as well as the recovery of the gold. The block-and-tackle idea had worked out well. The local blacksmith had spent some time in the Pacific Northwest as a lumberjack, and he knew considerable about rigging pulleys and slings and working high up like that. The recovery effort had taken most of the day, but now the gold was safe and sound.

Longarm knew that, but something drew him toward the bank anyway, some restless part of his personality that allowed him to take nothing for granted. He left Mrs.

Hingerson's and strolled down the darkened main street of Sweetwater City. The hour was late enough so that even the saloons were closed. The only sounds were the sighing of the chilly wind and a growl from a dog at one of the houses Longarm walked past.

He took out a cheroot and snapped a lucifer into life with his thumbnail The smoke tasted good as he drew it into his lungs. As big an uproar as the town had been thrown into during the day, all was calm again now. Folks around here would talk about it for a while, and then the spectacular events would fade into memory, one more story to be told to children and grandchildren. One more good yarn . . .

He was at the bank now, stepping up onto the boardwalk in front of the building. He was about to knock on the front door to summon one of the guards to let him in, when a sudden sound that was out of place made him freeze. The sound came again, faint on the night breeze the stamping of horses' hooves as they moved around nervously. And it came from the alley beside the bank, where there shouldn't be any horses, especially not tonight.

Longarm's hand went to his Colt and slipped it noiselessly from its holster. He tossed his cheroot into the street, catfooted over to the corner of the building, and peered down the alley. Not much moonlight penetrated there, but enough so that he could see there were no horses. The sounds came again, and now he realized they were at the rear of the bank.

Moving quietly and carefully, Longarm slipped along the alley toward the back of the building. When he reached the corner, he took off his hat and dropped it on the ground behind him. Edging an eye around the corner, he took a look.

A saddle horse and a pack animal stood there near the back door, their reins dangling. A faint line of light around the door told Longarm that it was open an inch or so. It should have been closed and locked up tight.

He swallowed the curse that tried to well up his throat. He was angry . . . angry at himself and angry at whoever was inside the bank trying to get his hands on that loot. With McKendrie dead, along with his men, and Jace Drummond as well, Longarm had figured that no one else in Sweetwater City represented a real threat to the gold. The townspeople all seemed to be solid citizens, and Axel Schermerhorn, for all his bluster and borderline lunacy, had a successful ranch and surely wouldn't risk it in an attempt to steal that money. Clearly, though, the temptation had proven to be too much for someone to overcome.

Longarm listened at the door and heard someone moving around inside the bank. He eased the door open and slid quietly into the building. This was a back room, with another door opening into the bank lobby. The light came from a lamp on one of the desks in the lobby. The wick had been turned down low, but it still cast enough of a glow for Longarm to be able to see the sprawled body of the man who had been posted here on guard. He was one of Schermerhorn's punchers. Longarm bent over and checked for a pulse, found one beating in the man's neck. He was still alive, and Longarm was thankful for that. Whoever was after the gold had clouted him over the head—Longarm could see the goose egg on the cowboy's noggin—but hadn't killed him.

Moving to the inner door, Longarm paused as he heard another sound. Whoever was moving around the lobby was *whistling*. He was an icy-nerved son of a bitch, thought Longarm. He heard a dragging sound, then a thud. Risking a look, he saw a man dressed in black standing over one of the other guards. The two remaining guards also lay there on the floor to one side of the vault. Longarm peered at them until he discerned the movement of their chests. Evidently the robber had knocked them all out and then dragged them into a pile so they would be out of his way and so that he could keep an eye on them as he worked. He went to the vault door and bent close to the dial of the combination lock just above the handle. Thick white hair was visible under his black Stetson.

Longarm could afford to wait now and see just how good this fella was. The man in black worked at the lock for several minutes, pressing his ear to the door, before he twisted the handle and gave a triumphant grunt as the door came open. He straightened . . .

That was when Longarm stepped into the room, trained his Colt on the robber's back, and said, "That's enough, Clete."

The robber stiffened in surprise. Instinctively, his hand moved a fraction of an inch toward the gun on his hip, but then he controlled the reaction. Instead of going for his gun, he lifted his hands and turned around slowly so that he faced Longarm. His features were weathered and craggy but still retained a rugged handsomeness. Despite his surprise, a grin tugged at his mouth.

"Well if it ain't Marshal Custis Long," Clete Harrigan said. "Didn't expect to run into you here, Marshal."

"I expect not. How come you ain't in Leavenworth, Harrigan? For that matter, what are you doing alive? The way I heard it, you were at death's door."

"I got better," Harrigan said dryly. He laughed. "Hell, I was never sick, not really. I just paid off that prison doctor to make Emily think I was."

"Why in blazes would you do a thing like that?" Longarm was filled with anger at the way Harrigan had deceived his own daughter.

"So she'd believe I was really reformed—and so would you—when I sent Floyd to tell you where the gold was." Harrigan shook his head. "Poor ol' Floyd. I didn't figure on him getting killed like that. I reckon he must have told you enough before he died, though, to send you down here. Otherwise you never would have gone exploring in Sweetwater Canyon . . . and you wouldn't have drawn Matt out of hiding."

"You knew Ben McKendrie was really Matt Rainey?"

"Hell, no," Harrigan said. "But I knew he had to be skulkin' around somewhere close to the canyon. He was a threat to me as long as he was alive, a threat to find that gold before I could come for it, and a threat to come after me for double-crossing him all those years ago. I figured the first thing I had to do was smoke him out. You and Emily took care of that while I was busy escaping from Leavenworth and traveling out here." Harrigan shook his head ruefully. "Took just about all the money I had to bribe enough guards to get out of there. But now I'm here, and right in there—" He jerked a thumb over his shoulder toward the vault "—is enough money to let me live like a king in Mexico for the rest of my borned days."

"You're forgetting something," Longarm said. "I've got a gun on you."

"But you wouldn't shoot the man who saved your life, now would you, Marshal?"

Longarm frowned. "What are you talking about, Harrigan?"

"Up there in the canyon, when that fella had the drop on you. Who do you think picked him off from the rim? Hell of a shot, if I do say so myself," Harrigan added proudly.

"That was you?" Longarm exclaimed in surprise. He had given Jace Drummond credit for shooting Dan Wilson.

"That's right. You see, Marshal, I was looking out for you. I didn't want anything to happen to you until you'd taken care of Rainey and got that gold down from behind the Hornet's Nest."

"So you *do* call it that. I thought you might."

"Well, that's what it looks like," Harrigan said. "I was

181

riding through the canyon one day and saw it and thought about how it looked just like a hornet's nest. That made me think about Shiloh, and while I was sitting there remembering, I happened to notice that there was a little cave behind it. I knew then and there that if I ever needed a hiding place nobody was likely to find, that was it." Harrigan paused, then went on, "I got to admit I'm a little surprised you tumbled to it so fast. I thought it would take you longer. Actually, I figured you might not even find the gold. All I wanted was for you to smoke out Rainey. But once you located the loot, I figured I might as well let you do the work of getting it down. I'm obliged, Marshal."

"You're still forgetting that I've got a gun on you," Longarm said heavily.

"No, I'm not. I just know you're not going to gun me down, because then you'd have to go back to Emily and tell her about how you killed her poor old daddy. You reckon she'd ever have anything to do with you after that?" Harrigan's right hand lowered a little, as if he was about to drop it toward his gun.

"Don't chance it, Harrigan," Longarm warned him.

"Besides, like I said, I saved your life. That's going to make you hesitate. Only man I ever killed, by the way. All those bank robberies, I never shot anybody. Rainey and some of the other boys did, but not me. The only life I ever took was in defense of a deputy United States marshal named Custis Long."

Harrigan's hand moved lower. In another second, it would be in position to make a stabbing draw . . .

The guard who had been knocked out in the back room suddenly stumbled into the lobby behind Longarm, rubbing his head and yelling, "Hey, fellas, somebody jumped me—"

Longarm's eyes flicked away from Harrigan, and in that instant, the bank robber's hand swept down to the butt of his gun. The revolver came out of the black holster with blinding speed. Harrigan actually got a shot off, but it went wild and thudded into the wall because Longarm's Colt had already roared. Harrigan rocked back as the lawman's bullet drove into his chest. His gun arm sagged. He tried to bring the weapon up for a second shot, but it slipped from nerveless fingers before he could fire. Harrigan fell to the side, landing on a desk and lying there for a second before he slid on down to the floor.

Longarm strode over to him and kicked the gun away, then went to a knee. Harrigan looked up at him, eyes wide with pain and shock. "Emily!" he gasped. "She . . . she didn't know . . . anything about . . . this . . ."

"Never figured she did," Longarm told him.

Harrigan's hand, covered with blood from clutching at his wound, reached up toward Longarm. "T-tell her . . ."

"I'll tell her somebody tried to grab the loot from the bank and got killed for his trouble," Longarm said quietly, so that only he and Harrigan could hear. "I'll get her out of town tomorrow, and that's all she'll ever have to know."

"Th-thanks . . ."

"Not doing it for you," Longarm said. "Doing it for her, so she'll never know how her own pa used her for bait."

Harrigan's eyes glazed over, and a final breath escaped from his throat with a rattle.

Longarm knelt there for a moment, head down, then took a deep breath and stood up. He holstered his gun and turned toward the guard, who still stood there rubbing his head and looking wide-eyed at the corpse on the floor. He pointed and said, "Who in tarnation is *that*?"

Longarm glanced back at Clete Harrigan. A lie wouldn't last long, but then again, it wouldn't have to. Just long enough for him to get Emily on her way back to Philadelphia . . .

"Somebody who pushed his luck too far. But that's all I know. I never saw him before in my life."

Watch for

Longarm and the Golden Ghost

302nd novel in the exciting LONGARM series
from Jove

Coming in January!

**Explore the exciting Old West with one
of the men who made it wild!**